Chad's Chance

Book 3 in the Emerald Springs Legacy

ELLEY ARDEN, author of *Battling the Best Man*
and *Crashing the Congressman's Wedding*

CRIMSON
ROMANCE

F+W Media, Inc.

Copyright © 2014 by Elley Arden.
All rights reserved.
This book, or parts thereof, may not be reproduced in any form without permission
from the publisher; exceptions are made for brief excerpts used in published reviews.

Published by
Crimson Romance
an imprint of F+W Media, Inc.
10151 Carver Road, Suite 200
Blue Ash, OH 45242. U.S.A.
www.crimsonromance.com

ISBN 10: 1-4405-7101-5
ISBN 13: 978-1-4405-7101-5
eISBN 10: 1-4405-7102-3
eISBN 13: 978-1-4405-7102-2

This is a work of fiction. Names, characters, corporations, institutions, organizations,
events, or locales in this novel are either the product of the author's imagination or, if
real, used fictitiously. The resemblance of any character to actual persons (living or dead)
is entirely coincidental.

Cover art © andreykuzmin/123RF and iStockphoto.com/gradyreese

To my boys, who make brotherhood look like a blast. Adam, Daniel, and Chad Whitman have nothing on Ando and Tuk.

Acknowledgments

Monica Tillery, Holley Trent, Nicole Flockton, and Robyn Neeley, how'd a girl get so lucky to plan, plot, write, and laugh alongside all of you? Thank you for everything. My only regret is we didn't get to do it in person, shut off from the world in a Puget Sound cottage (with a case of my homebrew). Next time maybe?

My editor on this project, Julie Sturgeon, did so much more than cross Ts and dot Is. She diagnosed the hero and heroine with gastrointestinal upset in time to get that nasty stuff treated. (Chad and Jen thank you.) She also made me laugh at every page turn. Again, I feel like the luckiest girl in the world.

Much appreciation goes to the folks at Northern Brewer, who make some of the best home brewing equipment available. I never thought this wine drinker could brew her own batch of honey ale … let alone that it would be not only drinkable but damn good.

And to The Church Brew Works in Pittsburgh, Pennsylvania, whose breathtaking architecture helped me feel exactly what my heroine, Jen Chavez, claims: brewing is a religion.

Chapter One

The end of the day was made for a cold glass of beer.

All the scrubbing, rinsing, lifting, and sweating made Jen's limbs limp and her mouth dry. It was a good kind of whipped, the kind that left no room for regrets or loneliness. In fact, when the hoppy flavor nipped her tongue and inner cheeks, it wiped away thought and left behind a sense of satisfaction. She still couldn't believe she could make such a beautiful beverage from scratch.

Jen sighed as she reached a heavy arm over her head and felt around the dark recesses of her locker shelf for her brewmaster gloves.

"I need to talk to you."

Her stomach heaved on an internal groan. *What now?*

Felix was a beady-eyed creep who only came sniffing around the back end of the microbrewery when he wanted to cause trouble.

"In my office," he said, spinning on the heels of his snakeskin loafers and using stubby-legged strides to propel him from the break room.

Great. She slammed shut her locker and followed him, her pink rubber boots making faint squeaks as she marched. The scent of fried food and burnt pizza crust wafted down the main hall, adding to her stomach's discomfort. All she wanted was a beer.

"Come in so I can close the door."

She glanced over her shoulder into the hallway, wishing to pull a passing waitress into the room. It wasn't wise to engage Felix without a witness.

When the hallway appeared like a gaping black hole, she rolled back her shoulders, lifted her chin, and exhaled. "I prefer we leave the door open."

"Have it your way," he sneered, and then he deposited his lumpy body into the ridiculously large leather chair behind his cluttered desk. "Chavez, we have to let you go."

Air ripped from her lungs. "Let me go where?"

He tossed her a lopsided look filled with pity. "We can't afford to keep two brewmasters, so we have to let you go."

"You're firing me." The words scraped against her throat until she thought she tasted blood.

Shit. She always figured she'd be the one to get the last laugh around here … when *she* quit.

"Bruno has more experience."

Barely. He was ten years older, but he had only a year of additional brewing experience on Jen. What really mattered to Felix was that Bruno had a penis.

"Bruno's IPA tastes like piss," Jen countered, wringing her hands and stepping one foot backward.

Part of her wanted to go. Part of her wanted to stay. She could fight this. With Felix's subtle sexual harassment and Alicia's toxic jealousy over any female worker who was in his company too long, it shouldn't be hard to get an employment lawyer to take the case.

A long and vindictive lawsuit flashed before her eyes. Why would she want to waste energy fighting them? To get her job back? Felix and Alicia wouldn't be going anywhere, and as long as they owned the place, Jen's life here would be hell.

"Gather your things, and I'll escort you out."

"No need," she hissed.

As she stormed back to the break room, emotion overtook her, clogging her throat, burning her eyes. The blockage made her heart beat faster. She'd worked her ass off for this job—literally—sweating body fat in an un-air-conditioned brew house, and this was her thanks. Those serving vessels out there were filled with *her* creations.

Jerking open her locker, she bit hard into the side of her cheek to keep the tears in check. She was not going to cry. Not here.

That would prove the very thing Felix and Alicia had been worried about all along—a female brewmaster was too weak.

She peeled the Milwaukee Brewers' schedule magnet off the back of the door and yanked her Colorado sweatshirt from its hook. Her purse was barely big enough for the checkbook-sized wallet and sunglass case she insisted on carrying around, but still she stuffed the magnet and as much of the hooded sweatshirt as possible into it.

She slammed her locker again but opened it back up and reached for her gloves on the overhead shelf. Empty. She must've left them in the brew house.

For a third time, she slammed her locker, opened it, and slammed it a final time. It was better than screaming *motherfucker* at the top of her lungs for the restaurant full of patrons to hear. Oh, she'd scream it, but she'd wait until she got home.

Storming out the other side of the break room with her weighed-down purse in hand, she chewed the inside of her cheek and fought the fury. She'd like nothing better than to stalk back into the office and launch at Felix, clawing his eyes out. It would be satisfying, but it would be ugly.

Jen had firsthand experience with violence. Giving into unbridled anger where a man was concerned would make her no better than her mother, so she would refrain—somehow. She'd bottle it up tight, get the hell out, and find another way to release the angry energy that was eating her alive.

When she threw open the door to the brew house, Jen froze. Earthy scents hit her nose, relaxing her raised-back posture, calming her pounding heart. She dropped her purse at the door's threshold and stepped across like a Catholic schoolgirl headed for confession.

Brewing was her religion; it cleansed her soul.

She cried—just a tear or two—because she didn't know when she'd see something this magnificent again.

High-polished silver vessels rose from the floor like the staggered pipes of a church organ. Her breath caught, creating a painful blockage in her throat. She'd brewed her last batch of Lovely Lady here. Had she known it was going to be her last, she'd have paid more attention, made damn sure every detail was committed to memory. And she would've tasted it—over and over again—until she couldn't swallow without thinking of her trademark honey ale.

She took in the room where she spent most of the last two years, the sense of melancholy heavy on her shoulders. As much as she hated the owners of this establishment, she'd have put up with worse if that was the only way for her make beer. Without it, life seemed impossible. Something else her mother's many men taught her. There was nothing like a tall one to tame the savage beast.

A pair of purple brewer's gloves on the top metal step caught Jen's eye. She'd come for those, not for gloomy memories. There would be other jobs. Maybe not in Seattle. Maybe not in a microbrewery with cutting-edge equipment like this. But there would be other brewmaster jobs.

She'd do whatever she had to do to find one.

• • •

Chad accepted the billfold and a to-go jug of Lovely Lady Honey Ale from the waitress.

"Thanks so much," she said, smiling. "Hope you stop back soon."

He would.

This escape from the chaos back in Emerald Springs had been nice. Between breaking up a fistfight between Marlon Miller, Adam's fiancée's father, and a waiter at the diner, and navigating Dad's impending retirement, Chad still had to get through Adam's upcoming wedding. He was trying to remain positive and supportive. Dad deserved to slow down, and Adam deserved to be happy. But getting from Point A to Point B meant too much family and family business drama. Chad didn't have the taste for that. He still didn't know if he'd ever acquire a taste for settling down and being responsible like he'd promised Mom he would do.

He preferred the taste of a damn good beer.

Touching his pinky to the cold glass jug the waitress left behind, he wondered how long a sixty-four ounce growler would last him. A couple weeks? Dad wouldn't be officially retired by then, and Adam wouldn't be married yet, so Chad would definitely be throwing back a few. The good thing was, when he ran out, he could escape to Seattle again. Next time, though, he'd visit the microbrewery without Billy. The glazed-over look on his best friend's face told Chad this outing had been too much too soon.

"Everything okay at home?" Chad asked as he signed the slip and returned his credit card to his wallet.

"I'm telling you. It's the cutest thing. She smiles when she sleeps. Molly says she's smiling at angels." Billy held his cell phone inches from Chad's face.

The newborn looked more like a hairless monkey than the offspring of Billy and Molly, but once again, Chad said she was cute. He'd said it at least a dozen times today—even when the critter in question puked all over his shoulder. Thank God he'd been wearing one of those towels.

As Billy returned his attention to the cell phone, Chad turned his head, dropped his gaze, and sniffed his shoulder, making sure …

When he glanced up, something pink beyond the glass that separated the restaurant from the brew house caught his eye. *Boots?*

He followed the girly boots to a pair of shapely thighs and an ass that made his back straighten. "Who the hell is that?"

Billy turned his head and said, "Probably the brewmaster" without a hint of interest.

That was okay. Chad had enough interest for both of them. His breath thickened as she bent over to grab a pair of gloves, testing the limits of those denim seams, and then faced the restaurant. Surrounded by steel, dressed in a black tee and jeans, with hair the color of a midnight sky cascading from a spot high on her head, she commanded the attention of every vibrating atom in his body.

She was gorgeous. And then she was gone.

Chad blinked, and Billy's voice registered in his ears. "You know what I mean?"

Chad didn't have a clue. He opened his mouth for bigger breaths. What the hell …

"Hey, man. You okay?" Billy asked. "You're bright red."

He nodded and lifted the growler of beer as he stood with purpose. "I wonder if they give tours. I'd like a tour."

"Nah, I can't. I … it's been three hours already. I gotta get home." Billy held his cell phone in one hand and his keys in the other.

Chad searched the restaurant behind Billy with hyperactive eyes. "Yeah, yeah. I understand."

He'd be back inside the building before Billy left his parking spot.

As they weaved through the dining room to the exit, Chad kept one eye on Billy so he didn't run the poor guy over and one eye on the brew house. Would she show up there again? Would she have reason to come out here?

"I appreciate you making the drive up and taking me out," Billy said as he held the glass door open.

"My pleasure," Chad said, deciding to devote the next sixty seconds to heartily seeing off his best friend. "You're a lucky man."

He meant it. Just because he wasn't cut out for the responsibility of marriage and family didn't mean he couldn't appreciate the trait in a friend. Now, the minivan? That was harder to accept. Chad couldn't even ride in it.

Standing alongside the metallic blue hallmark of family life, they hugged—mostly chest bumped—and back slapped. "Take care of those girls," Chad said.

"Will do. Drive safe. Thanks again."

For a brief second Billy wore the same silly smile he had worn in the huddle minutes before he launched off the line with reckless abandon, wreaking havoc on helpless defenders intent on sacking Chad … but then it was gone. With serious lines carved into his forehead, he focused on the side view mirrors, looked over his shoulder enough times to give Chad a sympathetic crick in the neck, and edged the minivan out of the too-tight space.

Cautious. See? That right there was why Chad would never make a good husband, let alone a father. It was exactly why he was struggling to find a comfortable place in the family business. That constant awareness of other people's lives depending on you cut a man's ability to take risks. Hell, it eliminated them.

Chad liked risks. The risks made life fun. But since Mom died he hadn't been able to take a single chance without feeling a little guilty that he was letting her down.

"Shit."

The expletive came from behind him followed by a dull thud.

He turned around to find the woman in pink boots crouched on the pavement amid what looked like a sweatshirt, rubber gloves, and the contents of her purse.

"Let me help," he said, setting the growler of beer on the pavement, unable to believe his luck.

He picked up the object closest to him, a Milwaukee Brewers fridge magnet, and chuckled. "You don't see many of these around here."

Brown eyes, wet and wide, lifted to his face. "It was a gift," she said, her voice raspy.

If he thought she was beautiful inside the brewery, then he had no idea what to call it out here. In the early evening sun, flecks of red emerged from her onyx hair. She blinked, studying him with murky eyes. *Wounded.* Lashes that were too long to be real clumped together with what appeared to be tears.

"Are you okay?" he whispered, not even recognizing the sound of his voice.

She nodded and slicked her pink tongue between pale lips. "Always."

Blood hammered through his veins straight to his crotch.

He grabbed a pen and a butterscotch candy off the pavement and held them in his open hand.

"Thank you," she said, scraping her clean nails over his palm as she retrieved the items.

His jaw clenched as pleasant chills radiated from his hand over his body. He couldn't seem to keep his attention focused on anything other than his body's insane reaction to this woman.

"I like your boots," he blurted, hoping the inane statement would reverse this crazy train.

She didn't look at him as she stood. Instead she hung her head, and he felt like a giant jerk for being turned on when she was obviously upset.

He was seconds away from asking if there was someone he could call to help her out when she jabbed a pointed finger at his feet.

"You need to pick that up and get it to your car." The rasp in her voice turned biting.

When he didn't move, she jabbed again. "Do you know how hot that pavement is? Would you set it on a stove top?" Her eyes never left the growler. "Treat it right or don't drink it at all."

Chad bent over and lifted the glass jug of beer. Her fierce protection of the item reminded him of where he first saw her.

"You're the brewmaster, aren't you?"

An agonizing sound stuck in her throat and she shook her head. "Not anymore."

She sidestepped him. Her boots made the silliest *thud, thud, squeak* against the pavement, and her ass swung like a porch swing in a windstorm.

He jogged after her. Had she been fired? It would explain the tears.

"Hey, you're upset. Let me help."

Her initial glance could've frozen Puget Sound, but then she looked at the growler in his hand again, and her striking features softened.

"Okay. You want to help? You can give me that," she said, coming to a stop behind his Jeep.

With her sculpted eyebrows lifted and her lips pursed, she looked serious, like they were negotiating something much more valuable than a twenty-dollar growler of beer. He didn't know how old she was, twenty-five maybe, but the shadows in her eyes told him life experience made up for whatever she lacked in age.

Whether it was a good idea or not, he wanted to help her lighten up.

Looking at the beer, Chad shrugged. "I don't know. You're asking a lot. I drove all the way to Seattle for this beer." Not exactly true. He was leaving things out, like the part about how he actually came to Seattle at Billy's invitation to meet his baby. Then again, he left out the part about wanting this beer when he offered to take Billy to dinner in the first place. In this case, what the other didn't know didn't matter … especially if it ended up in a good time.

An odd smile lifted one side of her mouth. "Really?"

That half-smile lit a flame. Chad hitched his free thumb in his jean pocket and grinned through a blast of body heat hot enough to cause beads of sweat on his back. "Really. It's the best honey ale I've ever tasted."

She nodded, sniffed, and glanced above him. Then she smiled—big and bold. When she looked at him again, the tip of her tongue touched the tip of her snow-white teeth. "It is, isn't it?"

Zap! His brain primed his body with all sorts of bad ideas, and she stood there smiling at him with a twinkle in her sultry eyes like she was game for every damn one.

A reasonable man would give her the beer and walk away, but not a cooped-up risk-taker like Chad.

"We could share it," he said, knowing he could be reading her wrong. Maybe she wasn't interested. Maybe …

She snatched the growler out of his hand. "Follow me."

Chapter Two

Jen parked her car, hoisted the jug of beer from the passenger seat and headed down the path to Conner Park. She didn't wait for the sexy smile and clear blue eyes that were following her, but she knew the man who owned them was there. His Jeep pulled into the parking lot seconds after she did.

This was probably the craziest thing she'd ever done. Scratch that. This *was* the craziest thing she'd ever done. The shock and pressure of losing her job must've short-circuited the cautious, skeptical part of her brain. She did not, as a rule, pick up strange men in parking lots and drag them off to dark secluded spots. But tonight, she wanted the distraction.

Reaching into her jean pocket, she slipped out her cell phone, typing a message to Mara:

> Rough night. At CP. Check in at 10. If u don't hear from me, u know what to do.

It had been their routine since college. More than once Jen figured the sense of security was false, but it was something to fall back on when common sense led them astray.

The rocks crunched beneath her boots, and a similar sound came from behind her. She fought the urge to turn around. There was no need for chit chat. She didn't care if she learned his name. She wanted to sit in her favorite spot, stare at the Seattle skyline as the world darkened, and drink her favorite beer. And then, when her body was all warm and fuzzy from the alcohol, she was going to take advantage of him.

She didn't think he'd mind. He followed her, didn't he?

"Hey, wait up."

She winced. Five more leaping steps and she'd be there. She refused to stop now.

"No, keep up," she called over her shoulder, noticing his faint, wavy shadow on the trees and bushes beside her.

Her heartbeat stuttered—apprehension and excitement all rolled into one irregular beat. She'd rather feel that than the crushing ache she'd experienced as she said goodbye to the brew house.

There will be more jobs.

She stepped off the path, around a boulder, and over a line of low-lying shrubbery to the giant tree that had witnessed some of her lowest moments. She'd always been more at peace outdoors.

With a hand to the grass, Jen sat and shoved the beer growler between crossed legs.

The mystery man stood beside her.

She glanced up at him as she twisted the cap off the jug. He looked tall as the trees, standing angled toward the city. One bulky hand was propped with split thumb and forefinger on his upper thigh, which was covered with faded denim that molded to his thick legs. The jeans had probably softened on his body heat alone. Jen swallowed a mouthful of saliva.

The breeze kicked up, carrying with it the fragrance of dirt and leaves. His shirttails fluttered, and her attention climbed upward to his sculptured forearms and the bulge of bicep beneath the rolled-up cuff of his lavender shirt. He looked strong and sure and … rich. A Rolex watch hung heavy on his wrist. *Interesting.* She'd never been with a rich guy before. She avoided them. Her mother had had enough for the both of them.

And yet, as Jen watched this one admiring the skyline, she couldn't help but think he was different from the shallow, egocentric men her mother was willing to hitch her gravy train to. Then again, maybe not. He probably thought he was "slumming it" with the curvy, Hispanic chick in funny pink boots. At this point, she really didn't care. This wasn't about finding her soul mate.

She didn't believe in those.

He looked down at her and smiled, and she could've sworn the setting sun momentarily reversed its course. *Beautiful.*

"This is … cool," he said in a softer voice than the one he'd used in the microbrewery's parking lot. "I wasn't expecting this."

"You were expecting me to take you back to my place."

He shrugged. "Yeah. I guess so."

"I might be acting stupid tonight, but I'm not *that* stupid." She raised the heavy jug to her mouth, supporting the bottom with her splaying palm, and breathed in the strong, sweet smell of honey. *Halfway to oblivion.* "Cheers."

Flavor exploded on her tongue: grape, mulberry, and a hint of orange most people didn't realize was there. She closed her eyes as she swallowed, letting the lusciousness sweep away the day's bitterness. Felix may have taken away her job, but he couldn't touch the talent that let her brew this beer.

When she opened her eyes, Pretty Boy was squatting beside her.

"May I?" he asked.

His face was as strong and defined as the rest of his body, with a hint of raised-brow mischief, too. She handed him the growler and watched him drink, noting the minute the beer hit his tongue— his eyes took an almost imperceptible roll toward the back of his head.

He groaned as he swallowed, and her nipples tightened.

"That's damn good beer."

The raspy words were further salve to her wounds. "Thank you."

"Do I taste coriander?"

"Maybe." She smiled at him and then looked away at the brightening city lights. "My recipes are confidential."

"They should be." He drank more.

She could tell he was drinking by the faint smack when his lips formed a seal around the jug. She faced him, watching the satisfaction play out on his gorgeous face, waiting with bated breath for a repeat of the moment when pleasure stuck on a groan in his throat.

This time when it happened, she shuddered.

Chills covered her body, and she reached for the growler, hoping the movement would scatter them. Too much desire made a woman vulnerable.

Vulnerable was not a word Jen wanted in her vocabulary.

"What's your name?" he asked as he relinquished his hold on the beer.

"Jen." She cut herself off with a drink.

"Nice to meet you, Jen. I'm Chad."

Wearing a watch like that, she would've expected something stuffier, like William or Charles.

"I take it last names are against the rules?" He leaned into her and lifted the growler off the ground between her legs.

A mix of spice, citrus, and man infiltrated her nose as he pulled away. Her mouth watered. If she designed colognes instead of beer, she would design something masculine and mysterious like that.

"There are no rules," she said, after a good, hard swallow.

"A lady after my own heart."

But she wasn't. Genetically, she couldn't be trusted with one of those. She was half floozy and half deadbeat. Either way, if she hung around too long, she suspected she'd do some damage like her parents always did.

Chad stretched out on the grass beside her, his legs reaching a point much farther down the hillside than hers would. Propped on his left elbow, he took the growler again. "How long have you been brewing beer?"

"Since college." It was a funny story, if she left out certain parts, but even the abbreviated version was probably more than he wanted to know, and it was certainly more than she wanted to give.

"Where was college?"

"We don't have to do this." He was just being polite.

The growler was approaching the half-empty mark. That meant they'd polished off thirty-two ounces. Kid stuff. She'd never get buzzed at this rate.

Jen chugged. Mara could pick her up and they could come back later for her car.

"I know we don't have to do this. No rules, remember? But I'd like to know a little about you before we …"

"College was in Colorado." She didn't want to discuss what they were or weren't going to do. "I majored in chemistry. Two guys down the hall bought a homebrew kit and couldn't figure it out, so I took over. I've been brewing ever since."

He laughed. It was the sort of sound that struck a pleasant chord and echoed long after the original sound died. "The abbreviated version, huh?"

She nodded, drank again, and held the jug out to him. "Better get it before it's gone."

He waved it off. "After the day I suspect you've had, it's yours."

The sadness returned, slumping her shoulders. She'd definitely had better days.

"Listen, I don't know exactly what happened, but brewing beer like that, I'm sure you'll find another job soon."

She grimaced. "If it were only that easy."

"Why isn't it?"

"Well, the whole vagina in a penis-run world." She nodded. "*That*."

He laughed again, and her skin littered with pimples from the inside out. She liked the sensation. It was a headier buzz than she'd get from finishing off this beer. Combined, they would surely make her forget her misery.

The wind kicked up, tossing her ponytail. The darker the sky turned, the colder the air around them.

She pulled her legs to her chest and wrapped them in her arms, letting the warmth of her folded body mix with the inner warmth from the beer.

"If you're cold, we could sit in the car."

Not unless it started to rain. She liked it out here.

"I'm good," she said. Besides, she could always warm up with him.

• • •

When the wind blew again, Chad sat up. He wouldn't admit it, but he was cold. This wasn't where he expected to be when he proposed they share the growler. Still, despite the dropping temperature, it wasn't bad. Now that the sun had set, the city view was amazing. And then there was Jen.

He studied her, huddling against the crisp breeze. She wasn't what he expected either. Beautiful and complicated, yes, but there was a hint of hellion in there. The mix turned him on.

"Did you seriously drive to Seattle to buy my beer?" She dropped her left cheek to her raised knees and watched him for his answer.

A simple "yes" might get him faster action, but his one-track mind had taken a detour. She was interesting, and she'd already been jerked around enough today. Honest conversation seemed like the honorable thing to do.

"Actually, I drove up to treat my buddy to a night out. He's a new dad. Getting a chance to taste the beer I've been reading about was an added bonus."

Getting away from the farm was too complicated a subject to mention.

Her gaze wandered, but her cheek stayed resting on her kneecaps. "Where'd you read about it?"

"A couple days ago, I read a review in *Homebrew Weekly*."

She smiled, a clumsy sort of grin that didn't look as though it would stick. It lifted her lips, but didn't reveal any teeth. "You're a home brewer," she said, picking up her head.

"I am."

"And here I thought you were a boob man using my beer to get to my body. You're really a beer geek using my boobs to get to my beer."

She shook her head, chuckling. It was a low and raspy sound that went straight to his groin. God, he loved the rush of taking risks.

Chad slid closer. "Honestly … I wanted to get my hands on both."

Her laughter faded, leaving a twinkle in her eyes. "Then what's stopping you?"

Half a second was all it took before Chad's fingertips gripped her jaw and tugged her face to his. When their lips touched she exhaled, smelling sweet like beer and warm like woman. Every inch of his skin tightened on a seismic tingle.

He brought his other hand to cradle her face as he tipped her head for a better angle, and she surprised him with an open mouth and eager tongue.

Matching her enthusiasm with a strong hold on her head, Chad swept his tongue deep inside her mouth to taste the honey and citrus. A gut-wrenching lust hardened him until it hurt.

His arms twitched on the need to explore the rest of her, but her hands wrapped around his forearms, holding him in place. He could smell the cool, earthy scent of hops on her skin, and his brain short-circuited on the intoxicating smell. With a groan, he deepened the kiss.

He pulled her closer, and she smoothed her hands up his arms to his shoulders, his neck. Her fingers played in his hair. Her tongue played in his mouth. A wave of recklessness crashed over him, causing him to push into her until she was flat on the ground sprawled out beneath him.

The growler fell with a thud.

"Shit," Jen whispered against his mouth. "There was a lot left."

"So what? You'll make more."

Her lips curved against his. "Yes, I will."

Her spunk and enthusiasm were almost sexier than her curves.

As they kissed, he smoothed a hand over her breast, circling the center until he felt her harden and heard her breathing hitch. Her slippery lips closed over his, dropped to his jaw, and moved over his neck. If the ache in his groin was any indication, this was going to progress to the main show fast.

He'd done a lot of crazy things in twenty-six years of risk taking, but sex outside in a public park hadn't made his list. As eager as his body was, they were both in jeans without a blanket. How would they even manage the act?

Further logistical thoughts didn't stand a chance with her hand rubbing up and down his distended fly, so he didn't try to sort it out. He covered her mouth with his again, welcomed her tongue, suckled her lips, and felt beneath her shirt until he had a handful of hot flesh.

She whimpered as he rolled her nipples between his fingers. It was a soft, sweet sound that didn't match her bold, outer shell. The contrast thrilled him, and he lifted her shirt over her belly, exposing her. In the low light, he couldn't see the details of her bra, just that it was dark—like he thought she was. But that sound had been so light.

He wondered what she would sound like when she completely surrendered.

With his mouth teasing her breast, he trailed his hands up and down her inner thighs, stopping at the apex to trace her sex through the tight denim. By the way she bucked against him, he could imagine her wet and ready.

Every inch of him was so swollen he could barely function to unbutton her jeans and release the zipper.

She whimpered again when he slid a finger between her folds, up and down, while he licked her nipples and kissed her chest. By the time their lips met, she was panting. He was, too. The mutual need cut off the blood supply to his head, heightening sensation to his bottom half. He wanted inside of her, but first …

"Park's closing. Move along."

A bright light heated the right side of Chad's face, making it impossible for him to put a face to the voice. With a surprising presence of mind, considering their pre-interruption activity, he yanked Jen's shirt over her breasts and open fly before he sat.

"Yes, sir," he stammered, watching the light and accompanying shadow move down the hill away from them.

Jen growled, still flat on her back. "Talk about a mood crusher."

The next thing he knew, she was fishing a ringing cell phone out of her pocket and standing.

She turned her back to him as she spoke. "I'm good. I am. Promise. I'm on my way now."

She fiddled with her clothes and then bent over for the growler. A second later, she was walking at breakneck speed up the path with the phone playing defender, stuck to her ear all the way to her car.

"Can I call you sometime?" Chad asked when it was apparent she was going to try to bolt without talking to him. He could probably be convinced to return to Seattle even more often if she was part of the deal.

In the faint glow of a security light, he saw her lower the phone to the space between her breasts. Something in the shadows on her face told him he wasn't going to like her answer.

"No," she said, frowning. "I mean, I appreciate this. I do, but it was just a distraction. I won't need one tomorrow. I'll be too busy job hunting."

She handed him back the empty growler. "Thanks for the beer."

He sat in his Jeep long after her headlights faded from the parking lot. He'd had a better day trip than he ever imagined. Maybe that was why he couldn't bring himself to head home yet … to his family, where he wasn't sure of his place, to his job, where he couldn't find fulfillment. Following Jen to this park had been a risk, but he'd never felt better.

If he could just figure out a way to bottle this satisfaction so he could guzzle it during long stretches of boring business and family responsibility, he'd be a model Whitman son.

Chapter Three

Chad strummed his knuckles against the stubby underside of his chin and listened to Dad talk about the strained relationship between their farm and the Sanderses' farm next door. It never ceased to amaze Chad that friendships could sour so fast. No one liked to talk about it, but how could they forget Dad and Joe Sanders were partners before a falling-out pushed Joe to walk away and open Split Acres? Chad couldn't forget. It made his ability to maintain a close friendship with Joe's son, Jacob, all the more surprising to everyone but him. Life was too short to hold stupid grudges. Colleen Sanders and her new husband, Alan, were in charge of Spilt Acres, now, and they were making dramatic changes seemingly overnight. Good for them. But Dad and Adam were way too straight-lined and traditional to feel comfortable with that level of risk-taking right next door.

Nobody knew that better than Chad, whose earlier, acceptable risks on the athletic field gave way to worry about his hard-partying college lifestyle. Sure, he'd flunked out of the school of business and lost his baseball scholarship, but he'd found a school he liked even better and walked away with a degree in hospitality. He proved he could have fun and be responsible when it really mattered.

Lately, nothing seemed to matter, though. "Why would you want to retire in the middle of all this?" Uncle Sam asked, sarcasm apparent in his melodramatic laugh.

"We can handle it," Adam interjected. "Dad's earned the downtime."

Uncle Sam nodded. "I never said he didn't. I just can't imagine what a go-go-goer like Rich is gonna do with retirement."

"I'm going to travel," Dad said, smiling. "The world's a big place, and I've seen so little of it."

Because Mom got sick. They had been planning an anniversary Mediterranean cruise when she was diagnosed with advanced breast cancer.

Adam reached out and squeezed Dad's hand.

Chad looked away.

There was a moment of shared melancholy among the men at the corner table near the window inside Emerald Eats. Five years seemed like a long time when you were talking about most things, but not death. The pain of losing her still stuck like a jagged ball beneath Chad's solar plexus when the moment was right. Like now, when every breath was heartache.

He didn't know how much time had passed before he could easily fill his lungs again, but the half a club sandwich he'd eaten before the retirement talk started was now sitting heavily in his belly.

He breathed deeply just to remind himself he could.

"So, in light of everything, how can we help keep things on schedule?" Daniel asked, stretching one long arm over the back of the empty chair beside him.

Chad shot a look of thanks in his brother's direction. Keeping things on schedule would certainly lessen some of the drama.

Adam launched into a litany of tasks he needed to master before Dad's chosen date, none of which sounded particularly interesting to Chad. The right son had been tapped to helm the tea farm operations. When it came down to it, he found most of it tedious and boring, and Daniel—

Chad glanced at the stylish man lounging comfortably beside him—looked far too suave for driving a pickup truck and leading migrant workers.

The resort fit Daniel like the farm fit Adam. What about Chad?

He took another bite of his sandwich, letting the Swiss cheese melt on his tongue, and looked around the rustic diner that had been a Poplar Street staple since he was a teen. He used to drag teammates here for free food after football and baseball games. It hadn't changed much since then. The same mint green paint color covered the walls. The same black and white tile checkered the floor. The same oak tables and chairs cluttered the wide open space. In his time as manager, only the menu had been updated, and the refrigerated counter case and an industrial dishwasher in back had been changed.

There was something depressing about that.

While Daniel gushed about the eco-friendly changes he planned to make as the resort upgraded its spa and launched a line of tea-based bath and body products, Chad entertained a few changes of his own. For starters, he'd like to give the diner a facelift—take it out of the nineties and bring it into the age of bistros. He'd keep the rustic accents, like the rugged beams along the ceiling, but he'd add more steel, giving it an urban twist.

The menu would get a bigger lift, too. He'd keep recent crowd favorites like the club sandwich he was eating, but he'd add some vegetarian dishes to please the health-conscious, outdoorsy types who visited Skagit Valley on vacation. And of course, the ridiculous amount of tea on the menu would stay—he was a Whitman after all—but he was going to add beer.

Jen. The name roared through his brain.

For the past week he couldn't think about the beverage let alone drink one without seeing her face. A slow smile lifted his lips, and he covered his mouth with his palm. He hoped she was feeling better now. It was probably too soon for her to find another job, but maybe a microbrewery …

It hit him like a three-hundred-pound linebacker with a vendetta.

He wanted to turn Emerald Eats into a microbrewery.

Chad straightened as excitement warmed his face. He loved beer, brewed a batch a month at home. It was the perfect risk to take, one that would make his mark on the family business.

"Guys," he said, interrupting Adam's wedding talk. "I just had a lightning-bolt moment."

Dad raised his graying brows. Uncle Sam cleared his throat. Adam wrinkled his face. And Daniel grinned like he anticipated something hilarious and possibly bachelor party focused to tumble out of Chad's mouth.

"Go on," Dad said.

"How 'bout we turn this place into a microbrewery?"

Silence.

Dad sat back in his chair and folded his arms across his chest while he studied Chad. What had seemed like such an exciting suggestion floundered in the silence. *Here we go again.* He averted his eyes. Just because one little business idea didn't pan out shouldn't mean every other idea he had was doomed. Emerald Teas sponsorship of a NASCAR team could've been an awesome way to reach Southern tea drinkers. How was he supposed to know the team he picked was fraught with mismanagement and about to go under? Okay, so he'd finalized the decision on the strength of his friendship with the lead mechanic rather than on hard figures, but Buzz had been his *in*, and he'd needed to act fast. *You win some; you lose some.* And he wanted another shot at winning something big—like a microbrewery.

"I think it's a brilliant idea," Daniel said, breaking the uneasy silence.

Chad could always count on the brother who'd been his partner in crime when they were younger to encourage his whims. He could also count on Daniel to remain unscathed by the fallout. The guy was too smooth for his own good. He thanked him for the support with a smile, and then he noticed Adam glancing around the diner with a furrowed brow.

"Of course, you don't like the idea," he said. "I wouldn't expect you to like the risk." Hell, dealing with Dad's conservative approach to life had been bad enough, but then Adam came home and strengthened that practical side.

"It's not that I don't like it, it's just a major undertaking. Things are crazy enough right now."

Dad leaned forward and rested his elbows on the table. "An idea is just an idea until you have a concrete plan. How much thought have you put into this?"

Not much. But the longer Chad sat with the idea, the more he was certain he'd do whatever it would take to make it happen.

"Like I said, it was a lightning-bolt moment. It just came to me, but I'm serious about it, and I'll do whatever it takes to make it work."

"Then my advice to you at this moment is take some time and do your research," Dad said. "None of us knows enough about the sustainability of microbreweries to be pursuing this on a whim. We have a reputation to uphold, top-notch products made in a socially conscious manner. And after the mess of bad publicity the Whitman name received on the heels of the diner fight last month, we need to be even more deliberate and careful with our brand image."

Chad fidgeted while everyone stared at him. The fight wasn't his fault simply because he managed this place. Marlon Miller was a loose cannon, and Mike was a good waiter just trying to protect himself. Why didn't Adam catch any flack for not keeping his future father-in-law from attacking Mike and starting a chain reaction that ended with Colleen Sanders's new sister-in-law caught in the middle, and her face splattered all over the newspaper's front page? What was the big deal anyway?

He nodded, despite mounting annoyance. "I'll do my research, Dad."

"That includes hard numbers and talking to people inside the industry," Dad said. "Find an expert to help you come up with a solid plan. Then, we'll hear your formal pitch."

Find an expert, huh? Well, finally things were looking up. Chad didn't have to look far to find a beer expert.

Jen.

And people said lightning didn't strike the same place twice.

Now, if he could just find her and convince her to help him.

• • •

Jen lined her bills on the table in front of her. Thank God she'd already paid her half of this month's rent. That left car payment, car insurance, half of the utilities, student loan interest, food, and incidentals. With her savings, she'd be fine … this month. But if she didn't find a job soon, next month was anyone's guess.

If she came from a normal family, she could call her parents for a loan. But she didn't know if her father was dead or alive, and she'd be damned if she took a dime of dirty money from her mother, whose latest email graced the laptop screen when Jen closed out the bank browser window.

The top of her mother's head, cut off below the eyes, appeared beneath a single line of text:

Loving life in Punta Cana.

Jen didn't want to scroll down to see the rest of the picture, but like any good train wreck, the temptation was too strong. She hit the down arrow with too much force, and the keyboard shuddered. That was nothing compared to her full-body shudder when she glimpsed her middle-aged mother laying belly-down on the bow of a yacht wearing nothing but a floppy hat and G-string bikini bottom. A much older, tanner man with gold chains around his neck lounged in a Speedo beside her.

Jen slammed the laptop shut on a wave of nausea. It wasn't that she begrudged the woman an enjoyable life; it was just that Jen knew the morals she had to compromise to get there. Sleeping with a man in exchange for a credit card and expensive gifts made a woman a prostitute without a corner. And it wasn't the kind of thing a girl wanted to know about her mother.

"How's the job hunt going?" Mara walked into the living room with a mug in hand.

"I sent two more résumés this morning," Jen said, lifting out of her chair and joining Mara on the couch. "But no word yet from anything I sent earlier in the week."

"It takes time."

"I don't really have time."

Mara laid a lithe hand on Jen's bare knee. "I'll pick up your half of the rent next month."

"No."

"Yes."

"It's freeloading."

"It's a favor."

Jen huffed. She hated feeling out of control, powerless, and desperate. She'd charted her entire adult course to avoid those feelings that had been so prevalent during childhood. "If worse comes to worst, I'm asking your ex for a job."

Mara laughed. "I can't see you behind the bar serving commercial light beer for Mick."

"Me neither, but desperate times call for desperate measures." Wasn't that what her mother always said in defense of the morally corrupt life she was leading? Jen winced at the link. "Besides, it would temporary," she added. Not just because bartending sucked compared to brewing, but because Mick would use the time to drone on and on about how Mara should take him back, and Jen should help him convince her. That would end up driving Jen away.

"Well …" Mara sipped from her steaming mug, "maybe you'll get lucky before it gets to that point."

"Maybe."

Jen wasn't going to hold her breath. Luck wasn't usually on her side. If she didn't hear anything by the end of the week, she'd make something happen—even if that something was swallowing her pride.

"Hand me the remote," Mara said. "We might as well watch a movie while we can still afford Netflix, and you're off in the middle of the afternoon."

Jen smiled at her best friend's irreverent response to the serious situation and stretched toward the coffee table.

The shrill song of the doorbell made her freeze mid-motion.

Mara blinked. "Huh. Wonder who that is?" She set her tea on the table and got up to answer the bell.

"You don't suppose a job would just show up at the door, do you?" Jen asked, laughing.

More irreverent, jobless humor.

Mara opened the door, and Jen's eyes widened because standing on the other side was the guy from the park. *Chad.*

"Hi," he said to Mara. "I'm looking for Jen Chavez."

Oh my God! He knew where she lived. He knew her last name.

It was par for the week that she had made out with a psycho. She slinked down on the couch, using the back as a shield.

"And you are?" Mara asked.

"Chad. Jen and I met last week at …"

"Chad," Mara repeated in a sing-songy voice that had Jen's stomach bottoming out.

She hadn't given Mara complete details of what happened in the park, but she'd given her enough. He was hot. He was a great kisser. He was … standing in the living room, smiling at Jen, who was half hidden behind the couch.

Ugh!

Apparently she'd said enough to make Mara think she should ask him to stay.

"Hi," he said.

"I'm just going to take my tea and skedaddle." Mara tossed her a sly wink as she flitted out of the room.

Jen straightened with as much dignity as she could muster, which was ultimately impossible while wearing the tank top and flimsy shorts she'd slept in. Crisscrossing her arms across her chest, she took in his flawless appearance. Jeans like he'd been wearing the night in the park, another collared shirt with sleeves rolled to the elbows, and that shiny wristwatch.

It all added up to rich boy chic. And here she was half-dressed and struggling to pay her bills. She swallowed a sarcastic laugh.

"How did you find me?"

He shoved those hands she was intimately familiar with into his front pockets as he shrugged. "I got your full name from the review in *Homebrew Weekly*, your phone number from the hostess at the microbrewery, and then one of my father's associates used the number to look you up."

Why did that conjure images of organized crime?

She should be scared, but in his smiling presence she couldn't muster more than a little wide-eyed wariness.

"What kind of associates does your father have?" she asked.

"Not the kind you're thinking." He laughed. "Nothing illegal. We have professionals on retainer to run background checks when necessary."

Jen tightened her grip on her body. All right, *that* scared her. "You ran a background check on me?"

"No. Just a basic address search."

Which wasn't any more comforting.

"So you know all this stuff about me, and I know nothing about you." She shifted her weight to the other leg but maintained the stranglehold on her chest. "That doesn't thrill me."

There was mischief in his crooked grin, making her think he was twisting the words "thrill me" into something flirtatious. The idea of *that* set her tingling.

He stepped closer. "I apologize. It hardly seems fair of me to barge in here when you know so little about me." He stepped closer still. "Let me fix that. I'm Chad Richard Whitman, the youngest of three sons born to Richard and Shelia Whitman. I live in Emerald Springs, Washington, in a small house on the backside of my family's tea farm. I'm also the general manager of my family's diner, Emerald Eats." His grin grew into a blinding smile. "How's that? Are we even now?"

It was hard to say. There was a lot of detail in that mini-monologue, not the least of which was his last name and family business. Whitman teas were legendary in these parts. There wasn't a coffee house or eco-friendly restaurant that didn't sport the Emerald Tea double-leaf logo in their front window.

That explained the Rolex.

"My roommate drinks Emerald Tea Cherry Berry Spice," she said, figuring that was the safest way to acknowledge his impressive family ties without sounding too impressed. Jen didn't gush.

"Your roommate is a smart woman."

"She let you in, so I question that."

His throaty chuckle sparked amusement in his heavenly eyes, and she found herself giving in to a smile of her own.

"Did you find a job yet?" His expression turned serious.

Shoot. For a few minutes, thanks to this confusing conversation, she'd been blissfully unaware of her current employment status. She sighed and loosened her grip on her arms—just enough to keep the blood moving along, but not enough to expose herself completely.

He knew enough about her already.

"It's only been a week of searching," she said.

"I take it that's a 'no.'" He nodded. "That's good, because I want to offer you one."

She swayed at his words. "*You* want to offer *me* a job?"

Doing what? Despite the fact both drinks were brewed, tea was not beer and beer was not tea.

"I want to turn Emerald Eats into a microbrewery, but I need a solid plan to lessen the risk and convince my father to fund it. You know beer, and I'm assuming you know about equipment and regulations. Would you consider some contract work while you're waiting to hear about a brewmaster job?" Again, he hit her with the tantalizing grin.

It wasn't the proposition she expected when Mara let him into the apartment. Maybe that was why her guard dropped along with her arms.

"I need to know more," she said. "Where would I work? What would my hours be? How much would I get paid?"

"It's all negotiable." His gaze dropped from her face to travel the length of her body, creating a sexy pulse in his right cheek.

She felt the hot liquid weight of his perusal between her legs, and steeled herself against the onslaught of memories from their night at the park. It was a different time and different place, but she could feel and smell him all the same.

Working side by side with this man wouldn't be easy.

"Think about it," he said, slipping a hand into his jean pocket again, drawing her attention to the spot hidden behind his untucked shirttails. When he removed his hand, his fingers were wrapped around a green business card. "My cell number is on the back. Give me a call if you're interested."

He cleared his throat as she took the card, and then with a half-smile, he left. The abrupt departure was in tune with the surprising arrival.

What the heck?

Jen stared at the business card in her hand. She had bills to pay. He had a job to give. It seemed like a no-brainer.

But would she be able to maintain her focus when she was around him?

Chapter Four

Jen took the scenic route from Seattle to Emerald Springs. More than once a skinny road winding off into the rich, green trees made her hands itch to turn the wheel and explore. Despite all the years she'd spent in big cities, she'd always found more comfort in the quiet, uncomplicated calm of earth and trees.

But comfort wasn't something she was feeling now with her back sweating against the seat and her head throbbing behind her eyes. Maybe the desire to detour into the forest wasn't so much about spending time in solitary but about getting off the main road so she could turn around and head home—in the opposite direction of Chad Whitman and the job he was offering.

If she weren't so desperate for a paycheck, she'd have turned around long ago.

The end of the week came and went without a nibble at her résumé, and she was going through money faster than she expected thanks to needing new brake pads for the car. Her only options to make up the unexpected expense were to serve beer to drunks who would hit on her while Mick whined about missing Mara, or to give advice to Chad about opening a microbrewery while she struggled with her attraction to him. Considering the latter allowed her to make more money and work mostly from home, it was the better deal.

She hoped.

If she couldn't keep her hands off the rich guy who was helping bail her out of a bind, she'd be no better than her mother. And if she ended up no better than her mother, then the things Jen had been working for all these years, like independence, security, and self-worth, would be wasted.

Blech! Jen squeezed her mouth shut and weathered the nauseous surge.

Up ahead, a quaint, green sign with Welcome to Emerald Springs written in gold announced her arrival. She exhaled. She could do this. She could talk about brewing beer, collect her paycheck, and not compromise her principles. Not that she had a ton of them. But the ones she did have were important—they were the only good things that came from her childhood. Rationality, practicality, self-sufficiency, and inner strength. Anything her parents lacked, she cultivated as a survival mechanism, but it was a battle because they were part of her. She always anticipated lapses in control.

She couldn't afford one now.

The farmscape of the outer town changed to brightly painted, picturesque buildings lining a narrow main street. Growing up in Miami, attending college in Denver, and working in Seattle, Jen didn't have firsthand experience with small towns, but she'd watched enough television and read enough books to know the clichés. They were often down on their luck and filled with quirky people who couldn't keep secrets. Described like that, a small town wasn't a place she cared to be. But Emerald Springs didn't look down on its luck.

There. A faded wooden sign showed Emerald Eats on the right side of the street. Of course, to make her even more uncomfortable, she was going to have to parallel park with diners gawking at her from the front window. If she were in the city, she'd drive to the nearest parking garage and pay extra for her lack of parking prowess, but that wasn't going to help her in Emerald Springs.

She bit her lip, edged her Hyundai alongside a red pickup truck, and shifted into reverse. *I hate this. I hate this. I hate this.* She was going to have to cut it hard to fit between the pickup and the mail truck, which was slightly over the line into her space.

She prayed as she did, hoping she'd judged it right, wishing the people in the window weren't so damn interested in her.

Scraaaaaaaape!

The unmistakable sound of her right front fender against the left back bumper of the pickup prompted her to stomp hard on the brake pedal.

Heat rushed her throat and fanned over her face. *Shit. Shit. Shit.* Now what? No one was in the truck she'd hit, but she couldn't drive away and find a bigger spot before she found the owner because the diner gawkers would think she was a hit-and-run. She was going to have to try parking here again. And worse, after she parked, she was going to have to walk into that diner and breathe the same judgmental air as the open-mouthed people watching her.

This did not bode well for the whole working in a small town thing.

Three nerve-fraying tries later, Jen managed to get into the spot without hitting anything else but the curb. She sat in the car, staring at the black scrape on the pickup's bumper, knowing her car hadn't fared any better—with the way things were going, probably much worse.

Great. Now she'd be driving around with proof of her incompetence on display because her deductible was $500, and at the moment, she could barely afford gas.

Any thoughts she had of turning her back on the paychecks Chad was offering scattered on her next exhale. *Get it over with*, her brain said because it knew her well enough to know if she didn't confront the uncomfortable situation quickly, she'd feel worse and start looking for any reason to bail.

With her head held high, Jen walked into the diner and didn't once turn to look at the people sitting in the front window. Instead, she spoke to the woman behind the counter.

"Do you have a pen and paper? I scraped the car in front of me and I'd like to leave my name and number on the windshield."

That was how they handled things in the city.

The similar-aged woman gave Jen a snotty nod. "I do, but you should tell the owner yourself. Mr. Whitman owns the truck."

Of course he did.

Jen gave a self-deprecating laugh.

"Hey, you made it." The rich, warm voice hit her from behind.

She turned—slowly. As if she didn't already have enough ambivalence about being here, now she had to fess up to property damage.

Might as well get it over with. "I hit your truck."

Chad looked over her shoulder out the front window and laughed. "No, you hit my father's truck."

It just kept getting better.

"But don't worry about it," he continued. "That thing has more dents than a roof after a hailstorm."

She wasn't buying his nonchalance, and she wasn't going to forget about it. That was the irresponsible thing to do. She may share the same DNA as a world-class deadbeat, but she wasn't going down that road, too—even if the pull was strong, even if that part of her brain was telling her rich people could fix their own damn trucks, and she didn't need to be humiliated anymore.

Jen cleared her throat. "I'd like to talk to him." Which wasn't an accurate statement. There wasn't anything to like about it. Still ... She glanced around the restaurant in search of an older gentleman who looked like Chad.

"He's across the street with my uncle Sam, but he'll be back. Let's talk first, and then I'll call him in."

Fine. But one way or another she was going to own up to her mistake and make sure it was taken care of.

"Follow me."

It was a simple, expected request, but her feet dragged, probably because on the other side was a private audience with Chad. Even in the midst of coming clean about the embarrassing accident, she couldn't ignore her body's peppy-pulsed reaction to him. And that tiny bit of acknowledgment opened up a floodgate on Conner Park memories.

She'd made out with the man who was now signing her paychecks. *Niiiiice.*

Keeping a healthy distance between them, Jen followed. She wanted to erase her memory, but since that wasn't possible, she figured not getting close enough to feel or smell him was the smartest thing to do. She checked the theory with an inhale, and the only spice she smelled came from the nearby kitchen. Exhaling, she relaxed the muscles in her face. She could totally do this.

Chad glanced back, tossing her a paparazzi-worthy smile. "I'm glad you made it."

She gulped, unable to say the same thing, but her pulse picked up another notch and a wave of warmth smoothed over her face. Sweeping her gaze from the tip of his messy, brown hair to the curves of his powerful backside, Jen reminded herself to keep her guard up. She was here for a paycheck, not an orgasm—even though she had been cheated out of the last one.

She clenched her teeth and looked away from him.

The hallway was narrow and dim, dressed in outdated paneling and sporting framed team photos. Little boys and girls in baseball uniforms smiled back at her from behind the glass. Despite the Brewers magnet she refused to part with, which was a gift from her mentor, she wasn't a baseball fan. And these pictures represented a childhood she'd never been lucky enough to have.

A feeling other than frustrated lust expanded to fill her belly. It was the same old sadness she'd carried around her entire life. The saddest part was she'd carried it around so long it felt normal.

"Right in here," Chad said, standing aside an open door with his outstretched arm leading the way.

Jen nodded. She had to do this. It was a great opportunity to pay her bills and pad her résumé.

The Rolex glistened as she passed him, and she heard a voice in her head that wasn't her own. *He's a great catch.* Jen winced at her mother's voice. Jen wasn't trying to *catch* anything. She had a legitimate service to offer the man.

He closed the door and brushed past her on a cloud of soap and spice that littered her skin with goose bumps.

Legitimate service, Jen reminded herself as she stuffed her hands into her pants pockets.

And that legitimate service didn't require him naked—no matter how nice it would be.

· · ·

She hit Dad's parked truck.

Chad swallowed a laugh as he walked to his desk. She was a bit of a mess, wasn't she? That night in the park he thought it was the shock of sudden unemployment making her behave erratically, but the air of chaos remained despite her shiny, straight hair and business casual clothes. He was surprised she made it to Emerald Springs in one piece.

"How was your drive?" he asked.

"Scenic."

He smiled and sat. Getting her to talk to him wasn't any easier, either, which was probably for the best. Last time small talk led to … other things, and as much as he'd like to, he wasn't going to fool around with someone on his payroll *again*—not after he ended up with Tasha in his bed and an empty cash register in his diner. Shenanigans like that would only serve as a reminder of his historic irresponsibility and make his family question his judgment where this current project was concerned.

The microbrewery was risky enough already.

As clearly as Chad understood that, it didn't mean he could ignore his attraction to Jen or forget about what almost happened between them. Two weeks later, the dreams that involved finishing what they started had stopped ... but all bets were off tonight. Seeing her across from him with her wide, chestnut eyes and flawless face renewed his desire.

He was only human.

"So ... where do we begin?" she asked.

There wasn't a hint of lipstick on the puffy, peach skin she pulled between her teeth, which made her perfect for stealing office kisses without the risk of him returning to the restaurant wearing evidence.

He hid a grin behind his hand. "I figured we could start by having you take a look at the rough draft business plan." It was a lot safer than him spending another minute admiring her.

He spun the laptop around, eager to get down to business, but someone interrupted with a knock on the door.

"Come in," he called, expecting Dad and Uncle Sam.

Instead, Andie poked her head into his office, gave a quick, hostile glance at the back of Jen's head, and then offered a fake smile to him. "You're needed in the kitchen."

Somehow he doubted the legitimacy of that. He saw the looks she'd thrown at Jen when they were out in the diner. He clenched his teeth to block a frustrated groan. He didn't need Andie's usually dormant jealousy to awaken.

Nodding as the door clicked shut again, Chad offered Jen a shaky smile. "I'll leave you to look this over, and I'll be right back."

For someone who liked life fun and easy, at the moment, his sure was looking messy.

One foot outside his office, Chad glimpsed Andie waiting at the end of the hall. Maybe it was a coincidence, but his radar for trouble went off, so he closed the door behind him. It had been almost a year since he dated the sullen-faced woman, but she still got a possessive glint in her eye every once in a while.

If they were going to exchange ugly words, Jen didn't need to hear them.

Andie pushed off the wall. "Before you head to the kitchen, I thought you should know your father left. He didn't even come into the diner. He hopped into the truck with Sam and drove off before I could catch him." She huffed. "He doesn't know about the bumper, and I don't want that woman—whoever she is—getting away with what she did. Should I call Jacob and file a report?" Chad wrinkled his face in annoyance at having to deal with this. Andie had been an uncomplicated good time when he'd met her at a Fourth of July celebration last year. She was new in town and eager to make friends, and he signed on for the friends-with-benefits package. But he should've given it more thought because two weeks into hanging out and messing around, he learned she had a little girl who lived with an aunt in Spokane. That was the biggest bucket of ice water he'd ever had dumped over him. And then she started asking for cash. Chad gave her a job instead. He never touched her again.

After what Tasha did, employees were off limits.

"Calling the sheriff is totally unnecessary. I'll handle it," he said, keeping his voice even. "And for the record, that woman's name is Jen. She'll be working with me on an important project for the next few weeks, so when she's here, be nice."

Andie's critically arched brows regained their normal, relaxed shape. "Oh. She's an employee?"

"Yes, a contract employee."

She exhaled.

He ignored the hint of possessiveness in the mundane action.

"I just don't want anyone taking advantage of you or your dad."

Chad didn't want that either. Unfortunately, he wasn't sure it wasn't happening right now. Andie had turned out to be a good assistant manager, but it wasn't lost on him that her moods were in direct correlation to his perceived relationship status. It made things uncomfortable from time to time—like now. Still, he dealt with it because she'd needed the stability of this job to reclaim her little girl.

"I appreciate your loyalty," he said, adding a smile he didn't feel. "But really … there's nothing to worry about. Now if you'll excuse me, the kitchen waits."

Jen's fender bender was hardly a crime in need of Jacob Sanders's intervention. God knew the diner didn't need any more official visits from law enforcement. Besides, Dad wasn't even going to care. He wouldn't take a dime toward repairs. Richard Whitman was just that kind of guy. Still, Chad would tell him about the damage, so Andie couldn't cry foul and Jen's conscience could relax, and then he could get down to the business of opening a microbrewery.

Why was everything so damn complicated?

Regret swirled with frustration, creating a tornado of heartburn beneath his breastbone. He liked Jen. Under different circumstances he'd have enjoyed a run of fun with her. But if past experience had taught him anything, it was that he wasn't the most responsible judge of character—especially when it came to women. There was nothing like a hallway run-in with Andie to remind him of that.

Like it or not, he was going to have to keep Jen at arm's length.

Chapter Five

Jen knew beer, not business plans, but a surprising amount of competency emerged during her meeting with Chad. Her practical experience allowed her to fill in the gaps in his outline, and by the satisfied smile on his face, she could tell he was impressed.

She liked the way that made her feel: competent, capable, and surprisingly attractive.

Watching him set the stack of papers aside, she tried not to notice the sexy strength in his hands, because noticing that made her remember exactly how his hands felt sliding down her …

"Are you hungry?"

She swallowed the rest of her tawdry thoughts and nodded.

"Great. Let's go out and grab something to eat before we take a look at the property next door."

Anything to get her out of this closed-in space with him.

He chose a table by the window, and she picked at a hangnail when she glanced at her car. Mr. Whitman's truck was gone, replaced by a much smaller vehicle, and the absence multiplied her guilt. She didn't get a chance to tell him about the damage.

"Don't worry about it," Chad said. "Seriously."

He couldn't possibly understand where she was coming from. Taking responsibility for herself and her actions had been her only source of pride when she had little to be proud of and no control over the chaos. It defined her.

"I told you, I want to talk to him," she said. "I don't like the idea of him driving around unaware of damage I caused, or worse, knowing there's damage but not knowing who caused it. That's irresponsible."

His brown eyes narrowed and then glazed. "Okay."

When he leaned back in the chair and pulled a phone from his pocket, she held her breath. It was what she wanted, but being responsible was a lot easier to handle when you weren't staring down the barrel of the proverbial gun.

What if Mr. Whitman wasn't anything like Chad? What if he was mean?

Holding the phone to his ear but tilting it away from his mouth, Chad grinned. "You seemed so sure about it five seconds ago."

She found herself smiling in response to his teasing, despite her nerves. There was just something about this man that put her at ease. His lips, his eyes, his smile …

"Dad, I have someone here who wants to talk with you."

Jen's stomach pitched.

"No. That's fine. We'll be around."

When he dropped the phone from his ear, returning it to his pocket, she frowned.

"He's not far from here, but he's in the middle of something," Chad said. "When he's done, he's going to stop by."

Nothing like prolonging the thing she just wanted to get over with the most.

She lifted the menu off the table and used it as a distraction. But honestly, her stomach was too knotted to eat.

Apparently, Chad didn't feel the same anxiety. He ate enough for both of them, polishing off a dual-patty burger and heaping order of fries while she picked at her buffalo chicken wrap.

"Are you hoping for a job in Seattle or someplace else?"

His question was innocent enough. It was even loosely related to why she was here, but it was backloaded with something a bit too personal for her to answer easily.

"I just want a brewmaster job."

He studied her, his tongue sweeping over his lips, and then he smiled as he shook his head.

"What?" she asked.

"Nothing."

Oh, there was something, but the heat in her belly told her not to ask again.

"Come on. Let's take a look at that empty place next door."

Again Jen followed him, but they didn't get far. The woman from the counter stepped into his path.

"Jacob called in a to-go order. Talk about a coincidence, huh? Did you want to see him when he picks it up? Tell him anything?" Her eyebrows rose too high on her head.

Chad stepped around the woman. "No. Absolutely not. However, when my father gets here, you can send him next door. That's where I'll be." His words were clipped and growly.

Uncomfortable, Jen thought as she forced a smile at the women who didn't seem pleased with the conversation.

Chad didn't offer an explanation for the testy exchange, and her contract employee status didn't entitle her to an answer. So she followed him in silence to the messy, vacant building next door, all the while wishing there was an easier way to earn an interim paycheck.

"This place is the key." He swung an arm around the room with his hand, palm up. "It's currently owned by Colleen Sanders and was rented out until last month. I approached her about selling, and she said she'd consider it. I know it doesn't look like much in its current condition, but I think it's big enough to house some brewing equipment."

Jen scanned the open room from dusty bottom to peeling top. "How tall are the ceilings?"

He shrugged. "I don't know. Maybe ten feet."

She glanced at him as he stood with hands on hips, looking at the ceiling. The space above his head seemed much larger than four feet.

"How tall are you?" she asked.

He grinned. "Are you checking me out?"

"No." But still, she could've smacked herself because his teasing words had her eyeing him. "I'm trying to get a more accurate measurement of the ceiling height. You need at least fourteen."

"I'm six-one. What do you think?"

He was looking at her, a crooked grin on his face. Every so often, his gaze darted to the ceiling, and then back to her. She knew he was asking what she thought about the ceiling height, but there was a spark between them. While she tried to make a focused observation of the space above his head, coupled with some simple mental math, her brain wasn't playing fair.

What did she think? She swallowed a laugh. He was gorgeous in a rumpled but refined sort of way, strong and capable, but lacking the arrogance of a man who took himself too seriously.

"Ten feet," she mumbled, simply to say something in the hopes of halting her dangerous train of thought.

He glanced at the ceiling again. "Nah. I think you were right before. It's taller than ten." He walked to the back of the room and rummaged around in a pile of boxes. "There's got to be something in here to measure with. Even just a rough estimate."

He bent at the waist, giving her an A-1 view of his denim-covered ass. Holding a clammy hand over her mouth, she turned her back to him. She didn't need any more reasons to admire the man.

A step ladder was tucked against the wall in front of her. She figured it to be about five or six feet tall. At five-feet, three-inches, if she climbed to the top and reached the ceiling, then she'd know for sure he needed more space.

Halfway up the wooden ladder, Chad called to her, "What are you doing?"

"Getting a rough estimate." With her hands braced on the wall, she placed both feet on the warning label that advised the top step wasn't to be used as a step.

Sometimes caution was highly overrated.

The more Jen straightened, walking her fingers up the wall, the more the ladder shuddered, but at this point, getting down presented a scarier proposition than continuing on her shaky path. At least that's what she thought up until her right foot slipped off the edge of the step, and her squealed expletive mixed with Chad's shout.

She found herself wrapped in his arms, happy to be in one, unbroken piece.

She wasn't happy to be so damn comfortable pressed against him.

• • •

This did not constitute keeping Jen at arm's length, not when his nose was buried in her fragrant hair, his hands were flattened against her back, and his body hummed with the contact.

A half hour ago when her staunch sense of responsibility made her insist he call Dad, Chad was impressed with her integrity and hoped some of it would rub off on him—and help him keep his distance. Now, he was pretty sure the only thing rubbing off on him was her spicy perfume. His mouth watered at the smell.

Not good.

Still, it wasn't like he planned this. What was he supposed to do, let her hit the ground? That would hardly be chivalrous.

"Are you okay?" he whispered against her ear.

Her inhale was shaky, probably from the fall, just as his heart was racing from the sprint across the room. Sure. That was it. The physical contact couldn't possibly be to blame. Not if he wanted to get out of this situation without crossing a line that would make his family further question this microbrewery.

"I'm okay," she said, pushing her palms to his chest and tipping her face to his. "Are you?"

He nodded.

"That was stupid of me, wasn't it?"

It got her here like this, breathlessly pressed against him. Stupid wasn't exactly the word he'd use if he was being honest.

"Looks like you were lucky," he said.

Yep, that seemed much more appropriate. With her arms wound around his neck and her wide eyes staring up at him, he was feeling pretty damn lucky, too.

"Ahem."

Before Chad turned around, he knew the source of the deep, gravely throat clearing. He closed his eyes for a split second, knowing how bad this must look, but at the same time hating to surrender the closeness with Jen.

She did the hard part for him, backing out of his arms and into the ladder, her eyes now wide with something that looked a lot like fear.

"Dad," he said, facing the stoic man, conscious of his position: caught in the middle.

"Andie told me you were over here." The rigid posture and wrinkled mouth said he was confused and none-too-happy. "She didn't say why, though."

Chad squared his shoulders and dragged air into his nose. This wasn't the way he'd intended to propose the idea that the Whitman family should buy property from the Sanders family. In light of the current awkward situation, as directly as possible was the best approach.

"Colleen's willing to sell, and we need more space for a microbrewery."

Dad lifted his graying brows. "Getting a little ahead of yourself, aren't you, son?" He shot a quizzical glance at Jen, who was standing behind Chad.

He could just imagine what Dad was thinking? Exactly what Chad had hoped to keep him from thinking.

Damage control. He stepped aside, gesturing to Jen. "She fell off the ladder. She was figuring out the ceiling height. Fourteen feet is the minimum. We couldn't find a tape measure."

Dad stepped closer. "Young lady, are you okay?" There was concern in his voice but wariness in his eyes.

Of course there was. Dad was always so cautious. Unlike Chad, he'd been born with the perfect personality for a boring businessman who would never make a mistake.

"I'm fine," Jen said, straightening, but gripping the ladder until her knuckles turned white.

Chad straightened, too, pulling his shoulders back and lifting his chin. Regardless of how this looked, he'd done nothing wrong. In fact, by being here, he was simply doing his research, like Dad had asked of him. And catching a falling Jen meant he'd saved them the hassle of a workman's comp claim had she hit the floor instead of his arms.

"Dad, this is the brewmaster I told you about, Jen Chavez. She's in town helping me nail down the business plan."

Ever the gentleman, Dad offered a hand and a smile, but Chad caught the warning glance he threw his way.

"It's nice to meet you, Ms. Chavez."

"You too, sir. I ... uh ... actually wanted to talk with you sooner, because I had a little accident when I arrived."

"An accident? In addition to this one?" There it was again— that quick look at Chad that told him fall or no fall, Dad wasn't happy with whatever was going on here.

"I hit your truck with my car." Her face turned red, but she maintained eye contact.

The conversation didn't appear to be easy for her, but she followed through, owning up to her actions just the same.

He found that incredibly intriguing. The responsible people in his life stood up and spoke out without blinking. And because he couldn't do the same, he always suspected he wasn't cut out to tow any sort of line—so why tow one in the first place?

Maybe Mom had been right all along. Maybe he was just making excuses for screwing up.

Dad's brow furrowed as he rubbed a hand to his jaw. "I don't recall getting into an accident."

"Your truck was parked, sir. No one was in it."

"I told her it wasn't a big deal," Chad said, wanting to contribute something to the tenuous conversation.

"Property damage is a big deal," she said, flashing that determination at him once again.

"You're right. It is," Dad said, but the wrinkles on his face smoothed, and a smile tipped his lips. "I appreciate the conscientiousness. I'll also tell you that truck has more dents than a metal roof after a hailstorm."

Chad grinned at her and waggled his brows. "I told you so."

She exhaled as she nodded. "Regardless, I want to pay for the damage. Please, let me know what I owe."

Dad nodded, too. "When I have an estimate in hand, I'll contact you."

That wasn't going to happen. But knowing how important this was to Jen, Chad kept his mouth shut.

"You're bleeding," Dad said, lifting Jen's arm with a hand beneath her wrist. Sure enough there was a tiny trickle of red along the outside of her forearm—nothing major, just an over-glorified scratch. "We need to get that taken care of. There's a first aid kit back at the diner."

Jen looked up from the scratch, offering a weak smile. "It's not a big deal. Really. I'll just head back to the ladies room and clean it up."

When she'd gone, Chad wandered around the room, turning off lights amid the impossible weight of his father's silence.

Hopefully the tension would lessen when they were back on Whitman property.

"Let me lock up and then ..."

"So *that* is your industry expert?"

Chad blinked. "Yep."

"Chad ..."

"I know what you're going to say, but it's not what it looks like, and it's not whatever you're thinking." The minute the words left his mouth they sounded absurd. He'd had his hand down Jen's pants and his mouth on her breast just two weeks ago.

How could it not be what Dad was thinking?

Dad sighed. "She seems like a nice woman. Respectable. Responsible."

"She is."

"But you can't blame me for raising eyebrows at you finding a young, attractive expert."

The statement was fair, but damned if the lack of confidence didn't hurt anyway.

"How'd you find her?"

It was a simple question, but in a blink it could turn into the third-degree with Chad flirting with the truth about the night they met.

He fidgeted. "I found her at a microbrewery in Seattle." The less he said, the better.

Dad rolled his lips between his teeth as if it was taking a super-human effort to keep from saying something he'd regret, and then he exhaled, sounding defeated. "Please be careful, son."

He was trying to be, but, honestly, where was the fun in that? A careful man didn't take risks like opening a microbrewery with help from a sexy brewmaster. A careful man brewed boring organic tea and lived life like a monk. Chad did not want to be a careful man, but ... if the illusion got him what he wanted this time then he'd do his best to fulfill the expectation.

"I'll be careful," Chad said.

He didn't have a choice, if he wanted this microbrewery. After what happened here, Dad would be watching his every move, ready to pull the plug at the slightest hint of worry.

Chapter Six

Jen paced the hardwood floor, glancing out the window each time she reached the far side of the living room. Chad was picking her up today, and seeing him again had her bouncing around like she'd downed a gallon of his family's strongest tea.

She'd spent most of the week answering questions and presenting findings strictly by email—somewhat of a letdown after her visit to Emerald Springs. Despite her better judgment, she was crushing hard, and that didn't make sense. She wasn't a romantic woman. Men came and went from her life, and she didn't *pine* over them. That would make her too needy. Yet, here she was, stealing looks out the window, breathing fast, anxious to see the handsome, confident, funny man who was now—technically— her boss.

She'd never met a triple threat like him. Effortless humor was a rarity in a man, and it was a powerful aphrodisiac. Otherwise, she wouldn't be ignoring sound reasons for not getting messed up with the man who was now coming to Seattle so they could meet with a brewery equipment sales rep she'd connected with online.

A day spent admiring brand-spanking-new tanks and fermenters alongside a hot, funny guy? Cupid was jerking her chain.

But no matter how hot and funny Chad appeared to be, there had to be a catch. Everyone carried around unique, genetic Molotov cocktails. Everyone operated from a place of self-serving ulterior motives. Having never met a person who proved her theory wrong, she highly doubted Chad would be the first. It was depressing.

"You look nice."

Jen hopped away from the window just as Mara propped her guitar case beside the bookshelf. She was dressed in a sparkly tank top and puffy, knee-length skirt. The outfit wouldn't have worked without the teased hair, made-up face, and cowboy boots.

Mara had issues, too, but they were manageable and forgivable, and Mara said the same about Jen. That's what kept them together these last eight years. They were pseudo-sisters joined by a learned skepticism of other people's perfect lives.

They both knew the kind of crap that happened behind closed doors.

"Thanks," Jen said, glancing down at the yellow shirtdress she'd debated wearing. "But you look better."

Mara laughed. "For a gig. Imagine if I showed up like this to shop for brewery equipment. I'd look ridiculous."

The way Jen was dressed wasn't much better, considering she picked the outfit to make the impression on Chad she promised herself she wasn't going to make. Talk about ridiculous. But being thrown together in a professional capacity with someone who had his mouth on her breasts the first night they met was such a weird situation. She was bound to have some residual, flirtatious behavior because of it, wasn't she?

She smoothed a hand over the wide belt that accentuated her breasts and down the sunny, short skirt. The feminine getup had seemed like a good idea an hour ago when she was fantasizing about him to the tune of whatever random, drippy love song the radio threw her way. As she dressed, the idea of turning his head again made her giddy. Which was warped because Jen didn't do giddy, and she knew nothing could come from his boldest glance. If she took his paycheck and anything beyond friendly conversation, she'd be disgusted with herself.

She should change.

Instead, she stood in the same place, telling herself there was nothing wrong with looking good and feeling a little power trip if Chad said, "You look nice" or she caught him staring too long. She was convinced this was the right approach until the wicked voice in her head told her she was only doing what she came by genetically—throwing herself at a man because at the moment the rest of her life was a mess.

When Mara disappeared into the kitchen, Jen buttoned her dress up to her collarbone and fished a denim jacket out of the coat closet. There were certain lines she refused to cross, and anything remotely hinting at her mother's behavior was one of them.

When Mara returned, she eyed Jen's tweaked outfit.

"What?" Jen asked. "I might get cold. Those warehouses are drafty."

Mara smiled. "I like the jacket." She adjusted a glittery hair comb behind her ear. "I think Chad will like it, too."

Jen tossed a throw pillow in her direction.

She hoped she wasn't this transparent in his presence.

Thirty minutes later, sitting beside Chad in his Jeep Wrangler, she stopped worrying about what he thought of her because she was too busy thinking about him. Dressed in khaki shorts and a sky blue polo shirt with his light hair tousled by wind through the open roof, he was every college girl's home-on-break fantasy. She tried to take comfort in the fact she wasn't a college girl, but when he was around, he sort of sucked up all the air and made it harder to think rationally and behave like a reasonable woman.

She dragged her gaze away from him and focused on the nondescript, hard plastic dashboard. This wasn't the kind of car she pictured for a man wearing a Rolex. Then again, a worn-out, red pickup truck wasn't the kind of vehicle she expected for the patriarch of a wealthy family either.

Mr. Whitman. As far as men went, he'd seemed nice enough, normal, too. Nothing about his tanned, handsomely weathered face and simple oxford and jeans told her he was powerful and rich, but still, she'd gotten an off-vibe, like she didn't know the whole story. Which she didn't.

They were probably arrogant elitists behind closed doors, living in an ostentatious house, owning a veritable collection of luxury cars while average people like her struggled to keep one economy car running.

"How many cars do you have?"

Chad's brow bunched. "One. This one."

Hmm. She nodded. So much for that theory.

He chuckled. "Are you disappointed?"

"No." But she was a little surprised. "I'm just making conversation." She let her gaze wander from his strong side profile to the heavy watch hanging around his tan wrist. Maybe cars weren't his thing. Maybe he poured unreasonable amounts of money into toys like boats, jet skis, and all-terrain vehicles. She could see that sort of recklessness in him.

When she looked at his face again, he was looking at her.

He released the steering wheel and gave his wrist a couple of shakes, letting the watch slide down an inch and settling his hand on his thigh. Embarrassment twisted her insides until she fidgeted.

He was on to her.

"You expected something flashier, didn't you?"

She looked out the windshield, staring at the highway stretching ahead of them. "Maybe. The whole Emerald Tea thing got me thinking ... "

"That I'm rich." His voice was as tight as she imagined his face would be. Apparently her recognition of his family's success wasn't a compliment.

"I just ... never mind." She looked out the passenger side window, wanting to somehow put even more distance between them. She didn't have a lot of experience talking about personal stuff, especially not with men, and she wasn't going to push outside her comfort zone with this one.

His exhale echoed in the quiet car. "I'm sorry if I sounded harsh. I just don't see my family that way—especially not me.

We're over-glorified farmers, and the money that comes from that belongs to my dad."

Jen looked at him then because there was something in his words, something she had picked up on before. Humility, a bit of self-deprecation, and a willingness not to be pigeon-holed. It was all there in a single sentence … but the watch and last name remained. Could she look at him and not be bothered about money? Probably not.

It was a horrible thought because it meant she was seeing him through her mother's eyes—default programming. The bottom line was, he was rich, and she was the daughter of an opportunist who saw nothing wrong with teaching a little girl how a pretty dress and a smile could open a wealthy man's wallet. What would Chad think about that?

To think Jen had been fantasizing about something happening between them. What a joke.

Reality was so damn depressing.

She kept her hands folded in her lap and her eyes on the road. None of it mattered. For all intents and purposes he was her boss—nothing more. She needed to forget about what happened in the park, forget about the feelings he stirred, and focus on work.

By the time they reached the warehouse, conversation had normalized around beer again. It gave her some semblance of hope she could get through these next few weeks without making a mess of anything.

Then again, maybe she'd get lucky and find a job sooner—somewhere far away from him.

That was the foremost thought in her mind as she fell a step behind Chad and Marty, the brewing equipment sales rep, while they walked the warehouse aisle. The distance provided peace and quiet. Besides, it had been a couple of weeks since she'd been up close and personal with gleaming vessels like this.

Jen lost herself in her distorted reflection on the shiny surfaces. *Mash tun, lauter tun, wort kettle.* She listed them like lyrics of a song as she passed.

She just wanted to brew again. Desperation weighed heavily on her shoulders. In that moment, she knew if Felix called and asked her back, she'd go. It would be better than this "dry" limbo she was living in.

"The lauter tun separates solids from liquids," Marty said.

That simple statement perked up Jen's ears. The lauter tun did so much more than separate.

Annoyed by the cursory explanation of a critical piece of the brewing system, she stopped and pretended to study a fermenter on her right. She wanted to say something, but Chad didn't need her waxing poetic about equipment while Marty was giving his sales pitch. She'd give Chad the opinion he was paying her for later … when he wasn't on his, um, knees—correction—when he wasn't *crawling* beneath the lauter tun tank.

Her heart lodged in her throat.

The air around her heated so much, she grabbed the denim coat by the collar and pulled it wider across her shoulders.

It wasn't that his shorts spread across his butt and thighs like peanut butter gracing toast. It wasn't that the muscles in his forearms rippled and flexed beneath his weight. Those things were … *ah*-mazing but—she let the jacket drop to the crooks of her elbows—it was his face that did her in.

Lines of inquisition carved into his forehead. Interest sparkled in his eyes. And his lips parted as he peered up at the bottom of the tank.

She knew exactly what that sort of reverence felt like … tingly, breathless, pre-orgasmic.

She clamped a hand over her mouth.

"Jen, check this out."

She tripped. Over her own two feet. Probably because her brain was too busy processing everything, including him lounging beneath the lauter tun like it was a reconditioned muscle car.

Idiot.

Fortunately, she remained upright. With little more than an ungraceful flail of her upper body, she settled herself.

"It's a multi-outlet model," Marty said as he squatted beside Chad. "That allows for even drainage. You won't have to take the false bottom out after every brew."

It was all very rote. There was nothing special about the way Marty explained the product attributes, but still the sparkle in Chad's eye was magnetic, like the tingle of electricity between Jen's breasts.

"What do you think of that?" he asked, cocking his head and smiling.

What did she think? That she couldn't breathe between heat from the flames sucking the existing oxygen from her chest and her swollen heart blocking fresh air.

What was she supposed to think?

"It's cool," she managed, letting the jacket fall off her left arm and carrying it in her right hand. "It'll do the job."

He lay there smiling, propped on his elbows, reminding her of the night in the park. And—*damn it!*—all she wanted in the whole wide world was to crawl under the lauter tun with him.

Cupid needed to be shot with his own damn arrows. Maybe then he would leave her the hell alone.

* * *

She was gorgeous. Tan skin. Yellow dress. Black hair. And eyes that invited him to get lost inside her secrets.

It was such a strange time to be struck with the thought that Chad jerked to sit, narrowly missing his head on the edge of the stainless steel kettle.

"Whoa, there," Marty said. His laugh only heightened Chad's sense of foolishness.

Chad did his best to stand with dignity intact. Not looking at Jen seemed to help, so he stayed one step ahead of her the rest of the warehouse tour. It was weak and immature, but he didn't know what else to do. After his dad's warning, arm's length was no joke. It was the appropriate amount of distance between an employer and employee. That's what they were. But a minute ago, he was looking at her as anything but, and he got the heady feeling she saw him that way, too.

He was a fool to think they could carry on in a professional capacity without their very personal beginning complicating things. And yet, he'd been able to do it with Andie.

What was it about Jen that made her so hard to resist?

While Marty wrapped things up, Chad managed to maintain a conversation, all the while dreading the return to his Jeep. He'd planned to take Jen to dinner before he took her home. They needed to discuss what they saw, make notes of what might work.

He wanted to do *other things* now.

Chad may have shaken Marty's hand a little too hard on that thought, and then he may have walked a little too slowly to the Jeep because Jen was standing beside it waiting for him by the time he got there.

Her jacket was on, her hair disappearing into the collar, and she faced the street with an intensity that said she was being paid to study traffic flow. Even standing in a gravel parking lot with her back to him, her beauty overwhelmed him. He felt lighter, loopier even, like a kid with a new toy. Oh, the possibilities. *If she weren't your employee. If you didn't want this microbrewery enough to give a damn.*

The warning didn't pack the punch it had inside the warehouse. Out here with the sun speckling the earth, his common sense waned. He just wanted to have fun and feel good.

That had always been his default programming.

"How about grabbing something to eat?" he asked, knowing the question wasn't as innocent as it should've been.

She nodded but stared at the Jeep while he opened the door. "Thank you."

Her words were quiet and weak, and the lack of eye contact felt like an ancient form of flirting.

He was a goner, wasn't he?

Maybe he should put it all out there. Tell her how he'd made some mistakes before, gained a reputation for them, and didn't need to make anymore because he wanted the microbrewery—but he wanted her, too. With any luck, she'd turn him down this time, and that would be the end of that.

He kicked the front passenger tire as he passed. How pitiful was he? Daniel would be laughing at him, calling him a pussy for getting so caught up in one woman when the world was full of them. Adam would be telling him he should've hedged his bets in the first place by hiring a man and not someone who looked like Jen. They'd both be right, but he didn't need them ragging on him—for fun or in concern—now. The fact he couldn't control his own damn libido in order to see this microbrewery through without any disasters was no joke.

Maybe Dad had been right to worry about him.

Chad hopped into the Jeep and dialed his thoughts to making beer. That was the only thing that mattered here. He finally had something that mattered enough to make him want to be responsible and serious enough to achieve it.

"We should've taken notes," he said, starting up the vehicle and putting it into reverse. "I don't remember half of what Marty said. Hope you do."

Jen made a gagging sound. "Most of what he said was salesman bullshit."

He braked and dragged his gaze from the rearview mirror to level it on her. Sitting there in her sunny yellow dress with a single strand of hair skimming her face, she didn't look like she should be a cynical woman, let alone one who said "bullshit." That was the real beauty about Jen. She was unexpected.

He smiled. "Now, see, I would've bought whatever he sold me."

She smiled, too—bright and blinding. "I know. That's why you're paying me the big bucks … to make sure you don't get too excited and do something stupid."

Electricity split the air between them.

Her lips snapped shut and her eyes widened.

She felt it, too.

Without a care for the half of his Jeep hanging out of the parking space, Chad threw the vehicle into park. Something mischievous compelled him to give in, to misbehave.

"We already did something stupid, didn't we?" He leaned closer, setting a finger on her bare knee. Without thought, he dragged her skirt up an inch. "In the park."

"Yes." It was more breath than word.

He flattened his palm on her warm, soft skin. Time slowed while his heartbeat quickened. Nothing but breath between them.

He dragged his hand up her thigh, watching the movement, feeling an intense throbbing in his gut. "We shouldn't do it again," he whispered.

But he didn't lift his hand, and she didn't say a word.

Hypnotized. Mesmerized.

A horn shattered the silence.

Jen jumped, yanking her skirt to her knees, and for the second time in sixty minutes Chad gathered up what was left of his dignity and carried on, pulling the Jeep into the spot and then backing out again when the coast was clear.

Arm's reach wasn't going to work when it came to Jen. He was going to have to come up with another—more practical—plan.

With any luck he could bust out a solid idea for this brewery by the end of the week. As soon as that happened, he could get Jen off his payroll … and as soon as *that* happened, he could get her into his bed. It was as close as he was going to get to toeing a respectable line. And it would work. It had to.

Otherwise, he was going to do something stupid—again.

Chapter Seven

"This is a bad weekend for us." Dad was already two steps off the front porch and heading for the golf cart. "Between the engagement party and appropriating new field boundaries and Daniel under resort deadlines of his own, I can't make any promises."

Chad had no right to feel slighted by the tight weekend schedule, but he'd been so hopeful he and Jen could make their final pitch soon.

Yesterday's dinner had gone better than he expected, considering he wasn't at all certain he could keep his hands off her long enough to make progress on the business plan. With the help of a table between them, and her amazing ability to focus when necessary, they didn't just make progress, they finished. And what they had was *good*.

He hadn't ever been this excited about contributing to the family business.

He plopped onto the top step and watched Dad climb into the cart. He finally had a dream where his future was concerned, but it was going to have to wait. Adam was getting married and the other family businesses were in the midst of expanding. Those were serious matters, and serious matters came first.

Too bad serious wasn't normally a word anyone associated with Chad.

"Want to come with me?" Dad asked. "You can drive."

It was a nostalgic peace offering, but it was going to take a lot more than a ride around the grounds to compensate for the delay. He wasn't a little boy thrilled by a golf cart anymore. He was a man with a viable business plan ready for execution. Wasn't that what everyone always wanted him to be? Well, he was ready to give it a try.

"Yeah, I'll drive," he said, standing.

Joining Dad on morning field rounds would keep the conversation flowing. It might not be a formal business pitch, but it could be enough to make Dad realize he was serious and the microbrewery deserved more attention than the Whitman empire was giving it.

The golf cart had changed since Chad was a boy. They'd traded in the green one with balding tires that slipped over the rocky terrain for a red one with off-roading wheels. The scenery had changed, too. The trees were taller, the leaves were greener, and the ruts were deeper. But no matter how old he got, one thing would never change—he still wanted to stomp on the gas pedal and hit the biggest pot hole just for the fun of it.

He kept it slow and steady for Dad.

"I'm serious about this microbrewery. I need you to give me a chance."

"I know you're serious, and I have every intention of giving you a chance when the timing is right."

"The timing is right now, Dad. I don't know what else to say other than that I've never felt like this. I can see my future in this plan." For a microbrewery, not a life with Jen. Why did he feel the need to clarify that?

"That sounds wonderful, son."

Halfway down the bumpy, well-worn path to the orchard, they reached a compromise. If Jen could be in Emerald Springs this weekend—sort of on standby—Dad would do his best to gather Adam and Daniel and locate an hour between Saturday and Sunday to hear the microbrewery plan.

"Have her pack a party dress. You can bring her Saturday night."

Chad jerked the wheel a little too hard, causing the cart to shudder. Bring Jen to Adam and Zoe's engagement party?

"Unless, of course, you have a date already."

He balked. "I don't have a date, and she wouldn't be my date." Was this a test to see if he was being as careful as Dad had asked him to be? Or was he overreacting, behaving like a nervous high school kid when questioned about a pretty girl?

Dad sighed. "Listen. I may have been a little too hard on you the other day, and I'm sorry about that. I meant what I said. She seems like a lovely, responsible, young lady. I'm not insinuating there's anything romantic between you. I'm just saying she'll be here, so why not give her something to do?"

Chad tightened his grip on the wheel while he imagined Jen in a party dress, laughing, dancing, and drinking. There was only one place that was going to lead.

Dad had no idea what he was orchestrating here. Chad didn't need the encouragement.

"Penny for your thoughts," Dad said.

He'd always been too perceptive for his own good. Or was that for Chad's own good? How many irresponsible ideas had been thwarted by Dad's interruptions?

Not enough. He shook his head. "You know I don't usually turn my back on a good time, but I'm thinking with my track record, taking Jen to the party is asking for trouble."

And this conversation may undo any progress he'd made in the being-taken-seriously department.

Dad stretched his arm across the vinyl seat back behind Chad. They bumped along in silence for the longest time—enough time for him to gnaw the hell out of his tongue for saying anything in the first place. See? Impulsive. He should've kept his mouth shut. Some steely resolve would do him good.

"I only met her that one, slightly awkward time." Dad chuckled. "But when she insisted on paying for the damage to my truck, I got the feeling she's nothing like Tasha."

Chad was driving too fast, hitting holes in the dirt path too hard. The rush of the ride dulled the discomfort of talking about this and rehashing his past mistakes. He could've agreed with Dad, but he kept the words in his head. Jen was nothing like Tasha. Tasha had been brash and flashy, non-stop smiles and flirtation. When he'd been with her, it had been full speed ahead, so fast that it wasn't *if* they crashed, it was *when*. Jen, on the other hand, was responsible and dedicated enough to see this project through, despite the attraction. He'd never known restraint could feel so good.

"You know, the good thing about mistakes is when they're big enough, we don't usually make them again."

It was a nice thought, but what did Dad know about mistakes? As far as Chad knew, the consummate professional had never made any. "Thanks for the advice, but I think we're bound to have differing experiences here. You're just better at playing it safe than I am."

"I'm older, son. That's the only difference." He lifted his arm off the back of the seat and adjusted. "Believe it or not, I used to be a lot like you."

Chad chuckled. They had both played baseball in high school, but as far as similarities went, that was about it.

"Her name was Carissa. She lived across the hall from Joe and me when we were in college. Long legs, big blue eyes, and the voice of an angel."

Okay. This was not his father talking. He glanced at the smiling man sitting beside him. "Are you making this up?"

He shook his head. "Nope. She used to leave her door propped open while she sang and played guitar. One night, I walked over and ..." he cleared his throat into his hand, "talked to her."

Noooo. Chad side eyed him. That noise didn't mean what he thought it meant ... did it?

"Long story short, I ended up agreeing to manage her singing career. You know, so I could spend more time with her. I convinced Joe to help. I said it was going to make us easy money and be one hell of a ride. It was fun for a while. We booked gigs and drove her places. We missed a lot of class, too. I even considered dropping out so we could expand her fan base." Dad laughed, but when the happy sound died a heavy silence lingered. "Over Thanksgiving, she disappeared. Joe and I searched everywhere—even reported her missing when she didn't show up for scheduled gigs. Police found her living with some other guy across town like nothing was wrong and nobody should've missed her."

Missing classes? Quitting school? Okay, that was uncharacteristically reckless of his father. It sounded a heck of a lot like something Chad would do.

"You're surprised?" Dad asked.

"A little."

Dad grabbed the back of his neck and shook him gently. "That was one of many risks I took before I learned the benefits of slowing up and settling down. It'll sink in for you, too. The good things in life have a way of adding up until you have so much that unnecessary risk just seems like a good way to lose it. Cut yourself some slack, son. I'm proud of you."

Chad smiled as the words settled in his heart. It wasn't that he'd never heard his father voice pride before; it was just that when leveled at a moment like this—considering the magnitude of the things they were discussing—it felt more authentic than any number of compliments he'd received in the past.

He was proud of himself, too. This microbrewery was going to prove exactly what he was capable of.

"Just an FYI, I'm bringing Patty to the party." Dad finished the random sentence with a weird sort of throat clearing, like maybe the rest of what he wanted to say got stuck.

He backed off the gas, slowing the cart around a tree-lined bend. "I assumed Patty would be there." He didn't know what else to say. Patty had been a part of their lives for a long time, picking up after them, cooking for them, filling in when Mom was busy and then again when she got sick. Of course Patty would be at Adam's engagement party. But the idea of Patty going *with* Dad …

"She'll be my date."

Chad tightened his hands around the steering wheel and waited for some sort of anger or betrayal to set in—at the very least shock that his father would start something with a valued employee.

The wind picked up around them, but inside, he remained still. Dad with Patty was going to turn a lot of heads and prompt a lot of whispers, but apparently Chad wouldn't be among the shocked and bothered. Maybe that was because he had his own employee-employer relationship to worry about. Something else they had in common.

"I like Patty," he said, because it was true.

Who was he to judge Dad's decisions, especially when, at the moment, the man wasn't judging Chad's decisions?

"Thanks, son."

Chad nodded, swallowing against a lump of anxiousness in his throat. "It looks like we're both in for an interesting weekend."

•••

"I don't want to go." Jen stood with arms crossed over her chest staring at a pile of freshly washed and folded clothes.

"You have to go. I need the apartment." Mara shook the empty suitcase. "Now, come on. Pack."

Pack. So she could drive two hours to Emerald Springs to hopefully make a microbrewery sales pitch while she stayed in a house on Whitman family property for two nights, attended a family party, and …

"You know what's going to happen." The minute she thought about spending any time alone with Chad her skin pimpled.

"You're going to have sex with him. So what? You only live once."

Jen palmed her face and groaned. "That's only a valid excuse after a one-night stand." She groaned again. "And the fact that I think that makes me sound like a tramp."

"You're not."

"I know."

"Then pack."

Jen dropped her arms to her sides and stared at Mara. 'I don't have a choice, do I? He's paying me to be there for the pitch, and I can handle *that*. It's staying on his family's property and attending the party that feels weird." She closed her eyes so hard the muscles in her face tingled. "But his father was so kind about the damage to his truck, how can I decline an invitation that originated with him?"

"You can't, so pack." Every other breath, Mara glanced at her phone, reminding Jen she wasn't the only one with complicated man issues.

Jen sat on the bed beside her. "You really think giving him another chance is smart?"

Mara nodded and glanced at Jen with watery eyes. "Mick is a good guy."

"I didn't say he wasn't. But starting up when nothing has changed means you're either going to have to change your opinion about how many hours he puts in at the bar, or you're going to end up fighting twenty-four-seven again. You can't change him."

"I don't want to change him."

Yeah, she said that now. Jen shrugged and pitched a pair of socks into the suitcase. "Then enjoy your weekend." She couldn't change Mara any more than Mara could change Mick.

Mara gripped Jen's wrist. "You, too."

Jen scoffed.

"I'm serious. When was the last time you let yourself believe that something good could happen?"

Usually Jen didn't have answers to Mara's emotional questions, so she brushed them off with bawdy humor, but this time something came to mind.

"When I was brewing my last batch of Lovely Lady . . ." Jen's vision blurred as she stared into space. "I had this weird feeling that something wonderful was going to happen." It was a warmth and peace she'd never known, like something she couldn't see wrapped her up and held her close. God? Angels? She didn't know. She'd never felt it before or again. "And look how that turned out," she whispered.

A week later she'd been fired.

"Well, good things happen," Mara said.

Jen blinked. She wasn't going to hold her breath.

A phone buzzed, and Mara's body jerked, but then she sighed. "It's you."

It was. A blocked call lit up Jen's phone. Maybe it was about a job. She pressed a finger to her lips and widened her eyes in Mara's direction as she lifted the phone to her ear.

"Hello."

"Baby girl?"

Jen's heart splashed into her stomach when she recognized the voice.

She wanted to hang up. It was her initial reaction every time. But when it came down to it, she couldn't hang up on her mother. That's why she preferred contact by email. It was so much easier to hit delete.

"You're surprised, aren't you?"

"Yep." One word at a time.

Memories bombarded Jen. The last time they'd been in the same zip code. College graduation. Dear old mom hitting on married Professor Krem.

"I'm coming to Seattle."

"No." Jen was pretty sure the shout didn't remain in her head because Mara jumped to her feet.

Silence. And then the thing Jen dreaded most. The soft sounds of sniveling.

"But, baby, I *need* to see you. I'm … Anton deserted me."

They all did.

"I'm a mess," she continued. "Seeing you always helps calm me down."

Seeing her mother had the opposite effect on Jen. She grabbed a pillow off the bed and drilled it at the wall. She didn't need to be pulled down like this when she already felt like she was drowning in unwanted emotions. She held a hand over her mouth and closed her eyes. It was easy to draw lines and keep boundaries when there was little contact between them.

Two beeps sounded in Jen's ear—another call. She opened her eyes and looked at the phone long enough to see an unknown, out-of-area number. Maybe *that* was about a job. Whoever it was couldn't be worse than this.

"I'm getting another call. I'll have to call you back."

"Baby …"

Jen pressed *hold* + *answer*, knowing full well it would be a battle to return to that call. All the while, Mara waited with brows stitched together over her nose.

"Hello." Jen hoped to God she didn't sound as messed up as she felt.

"Hi, may I speak with Ms. Chavez?"

"Speaking." Calm, cool, and collected.

"Wonderful. My name is Gretchen Collier. I'm calling from Mountain Pass Brewery in Boulder. I got your résumé, and I'd love to fly you out for an interview."

What a freaking day.

• • •

Chad sat on the steps of his childhood-home-turned-office space. Now that he'd pretty much begged for a shot at solidifying this microbrewery before the end of the weekend, he was waiting for Jen. There was overwhelming anticipation for both.

He stared at the lush, green, tea crops beyond the gravel driveway. He smelled the sweat and dirt of boyhood summers spent exploring the uncultivated field, and then later harvesting it as a teen. The images had been bombarding him since the impromptu jaunt in Dad's golf cart, so he indulged, let them roll around in his head and quell his anxiousness. A solitary brown bird perched on a limb several feet away. A sparrow. At least it looked like a sparrow from what he remembered. It had been a long time since he accompanied his mother to the Puget Sound Bird Fest—and not just because she wasn't here anymore. He glanced at the cloudless sky. He'd stopped going long before she'd gotten sick. It had been boring.

The bird sang, and in the distance another bird answered. Over and over again. God, his mother loved this peaceful, repetitive life. Could he? Would he be happy here year after year doing the same damn thing? Dad seemed to think so.

He glanced at the house. When he'd lived here, he couldn't wait to get away and find some action. Most nights, he hadn't rolled onto the porch until dark—sometimes, when he'd been much older, not until sunrise. Then he'd climb the trellis and sneak into Daniel's open window, slipping off to his bedroom before anyone besides his brother learned he'd broken curfew again.

Everywhere he looked there was another memory of his restlessness. He studied the pillar beside him, where he could see a dent despite a couple layers of glossy, white paint. He'd been wielding a baseball bat, desperate to play but foiled by a rainstorm when he'd taken a chunk out of the wood.

That mishap was mundane. Others were much worse, like when he and Dad had pulled into the circular drive after Chad had been kicked out of college. Mom had been waiting on this very step with tears in her eyes.

He winced. He'd hated almost everything about the rigidity of college, but he'd hated disappointing her more. Of course, that didn't stop him from disappointing her again and again. It had seemed so easy to brush it off, saying it was no big deal, they'd get over it—fun was not a crime. Back then, he'd had lots of years ahead of him before he had to grow up and be boring.

Well, shit. He was here. Grown up and still battling with boring. But if Dad was right, and they had restlessness in common, maybe there was hope for him. This microbrewery was the key.

The door behind him creaked. "Honey, can I get you some tea?"

He was having trouble looking Patty in the eye since he talked to Dad and learned something was happening between them, which was unfair. So he manned up and faced her.

"No, thanks. I'm good."

Patty smiled and nodded in her gentle way.

If he didn't think about her with Dad long enough to get uncomfortable, he could see the attraction. Patty was even-keeled and constant, never complaining, always the same soft smile on her face. After the life Dad had, complete with back-breaking labor in the fields and the loss of his wife, Patty was the epitome of comfort.

"Okay. Well, I cleaned up, and I freshened the sheets in the old master bedroom. Your friend should be happy there."

"Thank you." Chad smiled his appreciation.

The screen door creaked, and he knew Patty was giving him space. He liked that about her, too. She didn't pry, probably because she knew too much already.

He settled his gaze on the fields again amid a wave of hesitation. Having Jen stay upstairs seemed like a good idea when Dad mentioned it. After all, it would make it more convenient with the meeting slated to happen in the offices right downstairs. But now Chad wasn't so sure. It seemed unnecessarily intimate. Face it: it was hard to ignore the irony of the woman he was lusting after staying in the same room where Mom had gripped his hand and begged him to settle down, be more responsible, and become a productive member of the family.

If she were still here somehow … if she could see … would she be proud of Chad, too?

A car crunched along the gravel drive, and he straightened his back, sliding his palms on his denim-covered thighs. *Ready or not.*

From the microbrewery pitch to the weekend spent with Jen, Chad had no idea how any of it was going to go. All he knew was that he felt like his future depended on the outcome of both.

Chapter Eight

For two grueling hours trapped behind the steering wheel, Jen thought about everything: a job interview, a call from her mother, a weekend with Chad. None of it mixed. Each one crashed off the other and made for such dissonance, her head pounded by the time she guided her car down the narrow gravel road toward her destination.

Eventually the leafy surroundings opened up a bit so she could see Chad standing on the steps of a big, white farmhouse with his hands in his jeans pockets and a welcoming smile on his face. Part of her wanted to lose herself in that smile, but the other part begged her to stay away—especially now with Mom wanting to visit and a faraway job possibility.

Jen smiled back—not at all feeling the expression—and reminded herself she was here for a paycheck … not for him. The party dress in the garment bag lying across her back seat was part of the weekend plan; seduction wasn't. It didn't matter what Mara thought. It didn't matter what Jen thought three hours ago, either. She wasn't going to sleep with him and strengthen this ridiculous, idealistic attachment. She was going to set her sights on something else—the job in Colorado. And she was going to figure out a way to handle Mom so this incessant heartburn would go away.

Bolstered by the reminder, Jen pushed out of the car.

"Did you have trouble finding it?" Chad asked, his strong, tan hand grabbing onto the top of her car door.

He was still smiling when she came to stand, stuck in between the air-conditioned chill of the car's interior and the warmth of his body.

She nodded and used the motion as an excuse to look at her feet. "I took a wrong turn just past town but figured it out."

"Good. It can be tricky." He lingered there, making it hard for her to breathe with the close proximity. "Let me get your bags." He released the door and walked to the back of the car.

Jen inhaled into the space where he'd been. Hints of him carried on the breeze, and she closed her eyes momentarily, sharply reprimanding herself to not be led astray. She exhaled as she bent over and popped the trunk.

"Are you nervous?" His voice was muffled.

She was nervous about a lot of things, with the headache and heartburn to prove it. "A little."

"Don't be." He slammed the trunk and lifted the suitcase. "You're going to do great. I have a good feeling about this."

She was glad somebody did.

"Welcome to Emerald Springs Farm." An unassuming woman wearing a warm smile and a floral apron wrapped around her waist waited on the porch. She waved. "I'm Patty. Richard sent me to welcome you. Come on in. We'll get you settled."

Jen waved back. When Chad moved closer, she stretched into the backseat for the garment bag and quietly asked "Is that your …"

"Housekeeper."

He looked funny, like he was holding his breath or steeling against something. Either way, he wasn't comfortable with the conversation—that or her bag was too heavy, which was possible considering all the shoes Mara insisted she pack.

"It's a long story," he added over his shoulder and under his breath as he passed.

Huh. Interesting. Some sort of secret or drama accompanied Patty, and maybe even more intriguing, Chad mentioned it to her, like he would share more later. Personal stuff, family stuff, non-beer stuff. Her face tingled as her heartbeat accelerated. It was a cozy thought, and yet … she couldn't reciprocate.

There was nothing cozy about her family, nothing she cared to share.

With the garment bag slung over her arm and her eyes on the woman holding the door, Jen followed Chad onto the porch. Her heart rate normalized, but the butterflies in her stomach maintained the jumpy beat. This weekend was all kinds of outside-her-comfort-zone. Pitches for serious money, fancy parties, sharing secrets, and a family rich enough to employ a housekeeper? She swallowed a rush of panic.

One and done. She would give her pitch, help Chad seal the deal, and then she'd be out of here.

But *here* wasn't exactly what she expected. The house was large but homey. Glancing around the entryway, which gleamed with glossy, white woodwork and green, textured wallpaper, Jen labeled the décor classic and tasteful ... like a family lived here. They had once. Chad told her so, but he stopped short of any great detail as to why they used it mostly for office space now.

"Let me show you your room." Patty smiled at Jen and then turned to Chad. "How about I take that ..." she held her hand toward the suitcase, "and you can make us some tea?"

She seemed to have more authority than a housekeeper should, and something else—something maternal.

Chad relinquished the bag and his posture relaxed, bringing the smile back to his face. "Thanks, Patty."

And then he was gone, down the long center hall, leaving Jen wondering about what she'd witnessed.

"This way," Patty said, glancing back once before her foot hit the wool runner on the steps.

She followed, a picture of Chad making tea in her head. Very domestic. Old-fashioned, even. And he didn't protest. In fact, he sounded grateful to be given the assignment ... by the housekeeper. *So odd.*

With one hand on the thick, wooden banister and the other clutching her garment bag, Jen puzzled over that. She wasn't one for personal questions, but being here and witnessing the interactions between Patty and Chad, she was even more curious about the man and the family behind him.

"It's a beautiful house," she said, because remaining quiet seemed rude.

"It is. I like it best on weekends when we have guests, because it feels like a home again." The woman reached the landing and faced Jen. "During the week it belongs to marketing and publicity. Their offices are on the first floor, and as I understand it, you'll be giving your big presentation in the old dining room."

Jen nodded and glanced over the balcony railing. It seemed like a nice place to work. And if the way Chad respected Patty was any indication, the Whitmans were nice people to work for. When she'd spied Chad's Rolex, she could have never guessed how wrong her assumptions had been. The Jeep, the pickup truck, the farmhouse. They might be rich, but they weren't flashy.

Of course, she hadn't met them all—yet.

"Right in here," Patty called from the doorway at the end of the hall.

Sunlight streamed in from two large windows on either side of a huge poster bed, making the white coverlet glow. Pillows piled high at the head of the bed, while emerald green towels were stacked at the foot.

"I changed the linens this afternoon. There are more towels in the bathroom closet. It's fully stocked with toiletries as well, but if you need something that's not there, just ask. What time would you like breakfast ready?"

Jen blinked. The woman was going to cook for her. "I don't know." And then she almost laughed because she sounded ridiculous. "I don't normally eat breakfast."

Patty smiled. "It's the most important meal of the day. You have a big weekend ahead of you. How 'bout I have it ready for eight?"

A warm, fuzzy feeling spread over her as she nodded.

"Pancakes and eggs sound good?"

"Absolutely."

It was like she'd stepped into another life, where someone cared enough to change her sheets and cook her breakfast—like the moms on the television shows that kept her company throughout childhood would do.

Patty laced her fingers together at chest height. "Excellent. Now, take some time to freshen up if you want. We'll be in the kitchen. Down the stairs. Back of the hall."

She closed the door when she left the room, leaving Jen in comfortable silence.

• • •

Chad had hit his wall. He couldn't stay in the house drinking tea and having cordial conversation any longer. But he'd promised Dad he'd stay nearby in case they could pitch tonight.

Slapping his palms on the kitchen table, he stood. "Let's take a walk. I'll show you around." Anything to get him up and moving.

Jen's brows lifted over the rim of her teacup, but she gave him a post-sip nod and stood. She carried her cup to the sink and paused with her focus outside the window.

"Patty is nice."

Chad took a couple steps so he could see out the window, too. Patty stood on the patio, talking to a farmhand.

"She is." It didn't seem fair to relegate her to an employee status after what he'd learned earlier that day, but it wasn't easy thinking of her *with* Dad, either. As a result, he had no idea what to call her. "Listen, she's not just the housekeeper."

Jen turned. There wasn't much space between them, which didn't seem to matter when he was inches from her back. But now it struck him as crazy intimate with her shallow breathing echoing in his ears and only charged air holding them apart.

Nervous energy rushed through his body. Bad timing or not, he wanted to kiss her, but out of the corner of his eye he saw Patty approach the house.

He stepped back. "I'll explain outside."

Before he could fully step away, Patty walked into the kitchen. If she questioned the intensity of the scene, she didn't say. She simply smiled and offered more tea.

Chad made their excuses. Jen said goodbye. And finally he was free. When he stepped off the porch and onto the gravel driveway, the bright sunshine burned his restlessness away. He relaxed and surveyed the wide-open green space. There were no rules of propriety out here.

Looking over his shoulder, he saw Jen taking in the surroundings with a quiet awe. Her eyes were wide, her lips were parted, and again her beauty captivated him.

"Is this all tea?" she asked.

He nodded, stuffing his hands into his pockets. "It is, but it's not the organic stuff. That has to be grown in a pristine environment." One that had far too many rules and regulations to prompt regular visits from him. "My dad started planting closest to the house as an experiment and expanded from there."

"It's amazing."

"Yeah. It's pretty cool. Thinking back to the way it was when I was little and seeing it now sort of blows my mind. He's a farming superstar."

Jen laughed. "Sounds like a reality show."

"Nah. It would be too boring. No skeletons in the closets around here." And yet, Tasha getting hauled off by Jacob in handcuffs when the theft was discovered and Marlon Miller brawling with a waiter during the dinner rush at Emerald Eats sure would've made for must-see-TV.

Jen looked up at him, squinting against the sun. "What about Patty?"

Chad blinked. He should've kept his mouth shut in the kitchen. Just because he wanted to address the Patty subject then, didn't mean he wanted to talk about it now. "Nothing terrible. She's …" He rubbed a hand across his mouth. What the hell. She was going to find out something was up at the party anyway. What if Dad and Patty held hands? "Apparently there's a romantic relationship between her and my father."

"Oh." More squinting. A tilt of her head. "That's okay, isn't it? Like, your father and mother aren't still married, right?"

"No. My father is a widower." It was easier to say it that way.

"Oh," Jen said again. She kicked a stone and it rolled ahead of them, veering off the path and coming to rest in the grass and weeds. "Are you bothered by the idea of them together?"

"No. It's just something I'll have to get used to." Like not having his mother around was something he had to get used to. Like not seeing responsibility as a noose around his neck was something he was trying to get used to.

Oddly enough, out here he could easily find peace. It had always been that way. The open air quelled his restlessness, like the whole wide world was big enough to handle him when four walls weren't.

They walked on. She didn't push for more personal information. She didn't ask a million questions about the crops covering the ground on both sides of them, and he didn't scramble to fill the silence. It was nice just being with her without any pressure.

Was that what had drawn Dad to Mom—and now Patty? Had they ever walked this road in an oddly slow but perfect peace? *Slowing up and settling down*, like Dad had said. Maybe this was the start of it. Not necessarily with Jen, but definitely with someone like her.

The trees caved in around them, creating a canopy overhead, and he had the urge to hold her hand. Silly considering their business relationship and all the complications that went with it, but he craved the closeness. His hand twitched, but in the end, he didn't reach out. He kept his hands in his pockets and his eyes on the dirt road.

Had it really been three weeks since he saw her on the steps of the brew house? Somehow she seemed like she'd always been here, sort of lingering in the peripheral vision of his life, like he'd always been meant to find her.

His jaw clenched because part of him dubbed that the most ridiculous thing. But then he glanced at her and didn't care how stupid it sounded. He'd walked this path alone too many times to count.

Walking the path with her was so much better.

He was about to say something, anything that might lead to a conversation about what could happen between them once they gave this pitch and the microbrewery plan was underway, but his phone rang.

Pressure built in his chest and excitement fizzed in his head. Jen stopped walking when he did, and their eyes met on a mutual thought.

"Maybe this is it."

Maybe by the end of this weekend, he could have the microbrewery and Jen, too.

• • •

God, he was such a nice guy. Jen bit her lip and faced the tea field while he took the call. She fought the urge to swat air at her face in the hopes of cooling off. It was just so intense, being here, seeing him … like this. However that was. She wasn't even sure. All she knew was he was a genuinely nice guy who treated people with respect, and that did something to her.

She held a hand to her chest and chewed the heck out of her bottom lip. Why was she being so dramatic?

Because she liked him. And not in the "oh, we could have fun for the night" way she'd owned up to over the past few weeks. No, this was like-like born of admiration and general wonderment, the kind that made a girl think getting to know someone better was worth the hassle because maybe, maybe he could be *it*.

She balked. She'd never wanted an *it* before. Relationships seemed doomed from the start, something you embarked upon because one or both people were needy and hoping the other could fix whatever was broken. She'd watched it too many times with her mother, and she watched it with Mara. *It* wasn't for Jen, and yet Chad made her wonder.

"They'll meet us at the house in a half hour." His hands landed on her shoulders, and her body had the gall to melt instead of tense, like those hands belonged there, like she wanted them there, too.

"Okay," she said, scrambling away, heading back up the road.

She couldn't have him. She wouldn't even know what to do with him. She'd never indulged in anything meaningful before. That involved too much sharing, compromising, and divulging. The opportunities for screwing up and being screwed over were endless.

"Hey." He grabbed her hand, slowing her steps. "You don't need to be nervous."

Yes, she did. If not about the microbrewery presentation, about the fact he wasn't letting go of her hand, and the longer her held on to her, heating her palm, stroking her knuckles, spreading the sweetest tingles over her entire body, the more she wanted what she couldn't have.

All of it—a mother who would cook her breakfast, a lover who would hold her close, and a life she could be so damn happy with and proud of, she'd never feel the urge to run away from who she was again.

Chad smiled as he squeezed her hand. "We're in this together."

He had no idea how badly she wanted that to be true.

Chapter Nine

"Looks like tea won't be the only beverage the Whitmans will be brewing." Dad stood and extended his hand. "Congratulations, son. And the fact you got Colleen Sanders to agree to do business with a Whitman in any capacity … " He whistled. "Icing on the cake."

A potent cocktail of pride and satisfaction washed over Chad, creating a buzz greater than any beer ever could. "Thank you."

He hugged Dad, letting the warm sensation from the joyful gesture consume him, and then he moved on to Adam and Daniel, doing the same. God, it felt good to be taken seriously. Who knew a business meeting could pack such a rush?

Dad opened his arms to hug Jen. "Growing our own organic hops is a brilliant idea, my dear. I can see the value not just to Chad's microbrewery, but to other breweries interested in going in a more natural direction. I must say, that was my favorite part of the presentation."

As much as Chad wanted to take credit for the meeting's success, after that it was hard not to acknowledge the presentation wouldn't have had the same impact without a comprehensive, forward-thinking business plan. There was nothing like seducing a farmer by giving him more reasons to plant and grow crops. The organic hops portion of the plan tied everything together. Now, Chad's desire to brew something that epitomized a good time meshed with Dad's desire to have a stable, multi-faceted family farm.

Without a thought other than supreme gratitude, he wrapped her in his arms, whispering thank you after thank you into her fragrant hair.

"I do hope you'll consider staying on as brewmaster," Dad said.

Chad's blood still hummed from the adrenaline of a successful presentation. But now there was more—a flash of clarity. Jen needed a job doing what she loved. Why shouldn't she brew in the microbrewery she helped create?

She tensed beneath his hands and pushed away with considerable force.

"Thank you," she said, rushing the words as she nodded. "I, uh, appreciate that offer. I have another offer, though, so I need to consider carefully."

"Of course," Dad said without a hint of the anxiety Chad was feeling.

All that adrenaline bottomed out in the pit of Chad's stomach, weighing him down, making his heartbeat hollow.

What other offer? Jen hadn't mentioned anything to him. Not that she was required to, but still.

"I've got to bolt," Adam said. "Zoe has a million things that need crossed off the honey-do list before tomorrow night."

"You poor sucker," Daniel said with a laugh as he backed off the porch, hands raised. "I'll be sure to think of you neck-deep in ribbons and pastries while I'm drinking beer and holding a handful of aces."

With a fake smile, Chad went through the motions of teasing his brothers and saying goodbye. Then he followed everyone out of the presentation room to the front door. A minute ago he felt like he might explode from happiness—before Jen announced she was considering a job elsewhere. Now it was like someone stuck a pin in him.

He was losing air fast.

Dad nudged his arm. "Tonight, you celebrate. You've earned it." He flashed a smile at Jen.

Chad felt buoyed by pride again. He'd never realized how good it would feel to bring something equally as impressive as what his brothers brought to the Whitman family business table.

From the top step, he watched Daniel get into his car, and Dad and Adam climb into Dad's truck. The powerful sense of right lingered as they drove away. The reason for the sureness hit Chad as the vehicles faded into the distance—he was finally seeing the kind of future he was capable of.

His next thought was of Jen.

She stood near the door wrapped in her arms. A faint smile graced her lips when he first turned around, but it vanished when their eyes connected.

"Congratulations," she whispered.

He nodded. "You, too. I didn't know you had a job offer." He tried his best to sound nonchalant.

"It just came up. It's not actually an offer, yet. I've been invited to interview next week."

That irked him. His father had offered her a job, but she held that offer in the same regard as some random interview that may or may not result in a position?

"Where?" he asked, feeling his composure slip with a too-tight voice.

"Colorado."

His gut contracted, which was stupid. She'd done what she came to do. Why did he want more? In the grand scheme of things, he barely knew her.

And if she took a job in Colorado, he never would.

"Jen ..." He stepped toward her.

She stepped back. "You know, really, I should go. It's silly for me to stay. I could make it back to Seattle tonight—be out of everyone's hair. You don't need me to ... "

He closed the gap between them, forcing her against the cedar siding of the house. He didn't care if Patty opened the front door. He didn't care if Dad or Adam and Daniel returned. The only thing in this whole damn world that mattered now was her knowing just how much he needed her.

Chad slanted his lips over hers, taking a second to savor the sweet scent of her breath. It was the purest air he'd ever breathed, trickling over him to warm his mouth and soothe his soul. He opened for more, just a taste, a scrape of his bottom lip over her top, the tip of his tongue on hers. His hands gripped her waist and pulled her closer, fusing her there.

Colorado his ass.

He had two days to convince her that whatever was between them was worth exploring.

"You're staying here," he growled against her mouth.

She answered with an open mouth and arms around his neck—no argument.

He kissed her like he'd wanted to since they were interrupted in the park. With tongues tangled, he laced a hand through the hair on the side of her head and leaned into her, using the house to hold them up. It was like every rush of adrenaline he'd ever chased, every shot of excitement he'd craved.

If Patty wasn't roaming around, he would've backed Jen through the door in search of the nearest bed.

"Maybe we should find someplace else," she said, sliding her hands to his shoulders and resting her nose on his, but she kissed him again before he could say a word.

He liked that, the battle between sensibility and urgency.

When they came up for air, her eyebrows bobbed and her lips curved. "You know, you own a farm. There are a million trees we could hide behind and not a single cop to interrupt this time."

He chuckled. "I have a house, too. With a bed."

"Classy," she teased.

But then something darkened her eyes. She smiled through it, and he wondered if he'd seen anything worrisome at all. He didn't have years of experience reading her.

Dropping his mouth to hers, he kissed her again. Softly. Sweetly. Because his mind was elsewhere, lingering on that moment of dissonance.

When it came to Jen, there was so much more to learn, and this weekend was the perfect place to start.

• • •

Chad's house was small, smaller than the apartment Jen shared with Mara. He said it had been a security shack before they wired the farm with cameras that fed into one central location. Somehow it suited him.

She studied the whitewashed, breadboard walls. They were bare. She liked them that way. A blank canvas. His furniture was minimal and modern. Attractive. Uncluttered. Kind of like him.

"So, Miami. What's it like?"

Jen winced, glad her back was to him. The small talk while he poured drinks was a bit unexpected after the intensity of what happened on the porch, but the drive over had cooled the burn. Besides, a little conversation was probably more civilized than going at it on the floor, and questions about who she was and where she came from were bound to happen the more time they spent together, which was normal when two people were skirting around a … she swallowed … relationship.

Not that it would ever get that far, but something had shifted today, something that made it seem possible. Maybe. But that innocent question about her city of birth conjured images of strip clubs and strangers passed out on her couch in an apartment not fit for the rats let alone a kid.

"Miami is hot and sunny." She perched on the edge of a gray sofa, watching him through the cutout that allowed access to the kitchen.

He glanced at her, two brown bottles in his hands. "I've never been to Miami, and even I know that. Tell me something only a native would know."

That there wasn't a more class divided city than Miami. That people with money like the Whitmans lived in Coconut Grove far away from people without money like the Chavezes.

"Natives avoid South Beach unless there's really, truly nothing else to do," she said instead, knowing it was lame. But it was safer than telling him about *her* Miami.

He laughed as he carried two frosted glasses of beer into the living room. "Come on, you're telling me beautiful people in bathing suits strolling the sidewalk isn't worth a daily trip to the beach?"

"It's not." She took a mug and held the glass to her face, breathing in the frigid air, hoping it would ice over her discomfort.

Through the cold she smelled a hoppy citrus, and she smiled. It didn't smell like something you could buy in a store. "You made this, didn't you?"

"I did." He was smiling, too, holding the mug up and out toward her. "To us. To our microbrewery. Cheers."

She touched her mug to his despite panic priming her joints and insisting she run. What was she doing here, pretending to be a normal woman with a decent guy? It was so ridiculous. And yet, even as her muscles twitched, she didn't stand to leave. She stayed, letting herself indulge in the biggest fantasy she'd ever had—because for the first time in a long time it was too depressing to run away.

"What do you think?"

That I'm crazy, but he was talking about the beer, so she drank, savored, and genuinely smiled at the taste lingering on her tongue. "It's good." She drank again. "You're good."

He raised his eyebrows and leaned in. "I can be bad."

She swatted his chest. "I meant you're good at brewing."

He laughed and straightened, sipping from his glass. "Thanks. I can be bad at that, too. I once forgot to add priming sugar, and then I didn't taste it before I shipped it to a friend as a wedding present. He saved it for the rehearsal dinner. You should've seen the faces up and down that table."

"No."

"Yes. The bride-to-be spit a mouthful all over her filet. She never did like me, and that was the nail in my coffin. She accused me of doing it on purpose."

Jen cackled. She pictured a bridezilla who probably didn't appreciate craft beer in the first place, getting a mouthful of flat beer. When she caught her breath, she wiped tears from her eyes and noticed Chad staring at her.

"Do you really want to move to Colorado?"

She fidgeted. "I want to brew beer." It was her rote answer, her safe answer.

"Then brew beer here—with me."

He set his mug on the coffee table and slid closer, smoothing his hand over her back, stirring simultaneous heat and chills.

God, why did she want what she shouldn't have? How could this possibly work?

"Chad, this is nice, but … "

"Nice?" he questioned in her ear, deepening the chills. "Puppies are nice. Flowers are nice. This could be … everything."

Could it? She had no point of reference for nice like that. Mara and Mick were as close as she got to witnessing a healthy relationship, and with the amount of shouting they did, that was questionable.

"I don't know," she said, even as she leaned forward, relinquishing her beer, and tilted her head so he could brush the hair aside.

He touched lips to her neck, and let his exhale scatter there. She shuddered.

"*I* know," he whispered. "Let me prove it to you."

She gripped his thigh as his tongue tickled her lobe. She moaned when his hand slipped across her breast, hardening her nipples. If this was all he had to do to prove anything to her, she was sold.

But she knew better.

The question was, did her survival depend on her being cynical right now? Could she pretend a little longer?

As if it had a mind of its own to answer, her hand moved up his leg to the apex of his jeans. The brazen brush of her fingertips against his hardened flesh would be the point of no return, and she accepted it, enjoyed the jerk of his body when she firmly rubbed him there, and then she turned her head to meet his mouth.

Hot and wet, breathy and breathless, urgent but painstakingly slow.

He pushed against her until she spread beneath him on the couch, his lips dragging over her neck and his hands pushing under her blouse. Emotions she couldn't name warred in her chest and head, causing her to thrash, grab, and hold.

She'd never felt more desperate, more raw, more painfully bare. She wanted the lights off. She wanted them on. She wanted her breasts covered. She wanted his hands there. She wanted everything and nothing.

She couldn't settle long enough on one thought to decide.

"Prove it," she said, harsh and demanding. "Make me see what you see."

Chad froze for a second, his mouth on her breast, his hand down her pants, and then he lifted his head and looked her dead in the eyes. "I see you … with me … like this … for as long as you'll have me."

She lifted her face to the ceiling and closed her eyes, holding back something that felt horrifyingly similar to tears, but then his mouth and hands continued their tour of her body and thought and emotion gave way to pleasure.

He had no way of knowing she was the kind of girl who didn't stick, and she sure as hell wasn't going to tell him now.

...

For the second time in a matter of minutes, Chad's phone rumbled in his back pocket. Whoever it was thought the reason for calling was important enough to call two times in a row. He considered answering, but this—Jen—was important, too. So he kept his mouth on her heated skin and ignored the urge to answer.

Seconds later, his home phone rang.

He managed to lift off her and sit with the help of some serious deep breathing.

"My cell's been ringing, too. I should … "

"Get it." She finished his sentence, still spread out on the couch, her hair falling around her face.

Leaving her like that was one of the hardest things he ever had to do.

He stalked to the phone on the kitchen counter. *Blocked caller.* He answered none too nicely, hoping it wasn't a mistake.

"Where are you?"

Andie. "Is there a problem?" He sounded like a jerk, but he was the boss, and his question would be answered first.

She scoffed, irritation all through the sound. He told himself to relax and cut her some slack—it did take him three calls to answer.

"The cops are here … again."

So much for relaxing.

"Why now?" He rubbed at the wrinkles pinching his forehead.

"Marlon showed up demanding information about Zoe's engagement party."

"Shit."

"Yep. He broke a plate, and this time, he swung at a guest."

"I'll be right there."

Jen was now standing in the middle of the living room. A strand of hair stuck in a haphazard loop on the crown of her head hinted at their interrupted event. His chest squeezed.

"That didn't sound good."

He shook his head. "It's not. Zoe's dad went AWOL at the diner again. The cops are there."

Now what? A minute ago he was damn near begging her to stay with him, but after a phone call like that, he didn't know. Should she go with him on official business? Should she stay here and wait? Should he drop her back at the house where Patty was no doubt keeping the lights on?

He pressed curled fingers to his forehead and squeezed.

"I can walk back."

He shook off the frustration. "No, I'll drive you."

This was just a little hiccup in the road. They still had tomorrow, and tomorrow would be perfect.

This time when Chad had the urge to take her hand, he did, and they walked together to the door. But unrest hounded him. He should've answered the phone sooner. The diner was his responsibility.

"I'm sorry," he said when they reached the Jeep.

She looked up at him in the glow of the landscape lighting. "For what?"

He honestly didn't know, but somehow it felt like he'd screwed up again.

Chapter Ten

Jen walked the same gravel road she'd travelled yesterday with Chad. She needed to do something to calm the nervousness that kept urging her to hop in the car and escape to Seattle without so much as goodbye. Her *job* was done here, but after this family had welcomed and accommodated her, and after the shift in her relationship with Chad, it seemed rude. So, she stayed, but that didn't mean she belonged.

At the moment, she didn't belong anywhere.

Mara was shacking up with Mick in the apartment. Mom was heading to Seattle. Where was Jen's safe place? *The brew house.*

But she didn't have one of those to run to now.

Kicking a stone, she stared at the dirt road and crossed her arms over her breasts to weather the cool breeze. Would she belong here if she took the job that Chad was so eager for her to take? No matter how many times she asked herself that question, no answer formed.

Her phone buzzed.

As she fished it out of her pocket, her pulse quickened. She hoped it was him.

I'm going to try to get out of here by noon.

Air fluttered in her throat, making a silly sound. It was his second text today, neither one longer than a sentence, but holy crap the things she could read into those few words.

He was leaving early … for her. That was a good sign. Right?

Without him here, without a face she could read, she didn't know the thoughts behind his words, and she still worried about the stress he'd been carrying last night.

Maybe he changed his mind about her being here … with him.

This was why she hated emotional entanglements. They weakened her.

She opened her mouth to widen the inlet, sucking air into her lungs.

K, was all she managed in return.

Jen walked on, stopping every so often to pick a flowering weed, but she didn't raise them to her nose for a sniff. She might be exploring this connection with Chad, but she wasn't sentimental enough for wildflower bouquets. It wasn't like she was harvesting them so she could launch into *he loves me, he loves me not*.

She threw the flowers to the ground.

Birds raced overhead, squawking loudly. She welcomed the company. Born and raised in the city, she had to search for solitude. But here, it was the other way around.

She'd never been on a farm before. If she stripped away the uncertainty and emotions connected with being here, she liked the place. There was a peaceful sturdiness to the land. Anything anyone ever needed to survive could be gathered here. Mr. Whitman must have recognized that fact early on, because the entire family lived off this land now, doing what they loved alongside the people they loved. They built something from nothing, and that something could sustain multiple generations.

There was so much to admire about that. Security, sustainability, longevity, connection.

They were novel ideas to the child of two people who didn't give a damn about anything other than instant gratification. The people who created her never stuck around long enough to see the results of what they sowed, probably because what they sowed was a mess.

Up ahead, a red pickup approached. She had a pretty good idea who was behind the wheel, even though she was more familiar with the back end of the truck. She should've stayed in the house.

Conversation wasn't her favorite thing, and as nice as the man had been, he still made her nervous.

The vehicle slowed to a stop. "Morning, young lady." He grinned, shades of Chad threading through him. "Where you headed?"

Whatever apprehension she felt about his approach evaporated when he smiled.

"Just getting some exercise," she said, rubbing her stomach through her T-shirt. "I had to work off calories from breakfast. Patty sure can cook."

"Yes, she can." He chuckled, warm and loving, everything a dad should be—everything her father wasn't. Jen looked away, along the side of the dusty, dented truck, feeling awkward again.

"Did you file a claim and get an estimate on the damage, yet?" she asked. It was an abrupt change of subject, but being responsible for her actions always managed to elevate her above the garbage from whence she came.

"Not yet," he said, grinning as he leaned his head out the open window a little farther and glanced at the side of the truck. "I don't mind waiting. The nicks add character. I can tell you how I got almost every one. It's living history, this truck."

It was old, that was for sure. Again, not at all the type of vehicle she'd expected for a rich man. But until she met Richard Whitman she never realized it was possible to be wealthy yet simple, too. Knowing him was undoing years of preconceived notions she'd gathered from her mother's escapades.

His arm rested on the window ledge, his weathered hand hanging alongside the dirty metal, and then his face wrinkled. "I take it Chad's at the diner."

Jen nodded, struck by the need to squirm against the trickle of sweat beading down her back. Talking to Chad's dad after what happened with Chad on the couch seemed seedy. The man offered her a job. Did he realize she'd been minutes away from sleeping with his son? If he knew, would he rescind the offer? Surely he wanted better for his youngest than a brewmaster with family baggage.

Richard patted the side of his truck. "Alrighty then, you enjoy yourself today. I'll see you tonight." The truck began to roll away. "If you get bored, find Patty. She'll be in and out of the house while she helps with party prep. I'm sure she can give you something to do."

They were so welcoming and accommodating—perfect, like a Norman Rockwell painting. She'd seen a few in her time with smiling parents, steaming food, and cute kids and pets. But she couldn't recall one with a gritty Miami girl like her.

Leave. It was such a common thought she was starting to ignore it, and that development was a little startling. Mr. Whitman asked her to stay on as brewmaster, but she wouldn't waste another minute debating the offer if Chad didn't want her here.

Had he been serious when he asked her to stay?

I see you … with me … like this… for as long as you'll have me.

She covered her mouth with her hand and weathered the shudder that came with the memory. They were awesome words. Nobody had ever said anything like that to her. But people said things they didn't mean all the time, especially when they were caught up in a moment.

She walked, even more aimlessly now than before. A paycheck brought her here. A job offer could keep her here, and yet she felt like she was interviewing for so much more … a life—one she couldn't possibly deserve.

What if she stayed, took the job, and whatever was between her and Chad soured? These weren't the kind of people she could up and run away from when pressure mounted. They were good, kind, and trusting.

Her phone vibrated too many times for it to be a text message. Dread picked up the hairs on the back of her neck. It was about time for Mom to call.

Jen didn't bother looking at the screen.

What if she stayed, took the job Mr. Whitman had offered, and Mom came to visit?

Tilting her face to the blue sky, Jen groaned. She had to find something to do. All this wallowing and introspection was going to drive her to desperation, and that was dangerous. *That* led to things like picking up strange men in parking lots, carting them off to parks after dark, and letting them upend her whole world.

She couldn't handle something like that again.

There had to be something better to do. Mr. Whitman said Patty could put her to work helping prepare for Adam and Zoe's engagement party. Chad hadn't told her much about Adam's fiancée, but the fact that her father caused a ruckus at the diner intrigued Jen.

In the Whitman's portrait-perfect world, it was nice to know they embraced someone who came with a little chaos.

Maybe they could learn to embrace her, too.

• • •

Chad rested his elbows on his desk and stared bleary-eyed at a spreadsheet. He didn't want to be here. He wanted to be with Jen, but that's exactly where he'd been last night when Marlon roared into this place, taking Andie by surprise and throwing punches again.

Friday and Saturday nights were the busiest nights at the diner. They would be even busier at a brew pub. He shouldn't be shirking his managerial duties now, let alone when he was charged with the operation of a multi-million dollar brew pub.

Swatting a hand at the paper, he stood and stretched his arms overhead. Still, he wouldn't have given up the time he spent with Jen. The battle to find balance between this newfound need to succeed in business and the desire to enjoy himself was waging.

Maybe some solid sleep would help. Dad always said a well-rested man had a good perspective.

He glanced at the clock. *Eleven fifteen.* Fat chance of that happening now … or later with the engagement party on the horizon. Plus, he wanted to pick up where he left off with Jen tonight, a thought that brought a much-needed smile to his face.

See? Conflicted. And how could he not be? He wanted her. He wanted a microbrewery. The sensible thing was to mesh the things he wanted, but she wanted some sort of proof that this was the right thing to do. Just like his family. Everyone wanted to limit risk and make certain things turned out okay. Maybe it was reasonable when talking about millions of dollars and livelihoods. But just because he could see that didn't mean he stopped wanting a steady stream of fun and excitement, too. He needed to find a balance.

And he'd found her. Jen fit neatly between both camps. One moment she was all business, the next she was writhing beneath him. If he could have her *and* the brew pub, then he could be happy doing what he loved alongside the people he loved.

Not that he loved Jen.

He roughed his face in his hands. He was getting carried away. He needed caffeine. Maybe then he'd clear his head enough to finish payroll, so he could cut out of here.

Once he was behind the counter with coffee in hand, he settled. Soon this place would be a construction zone, starting in the vacant building next store. The two-tiered approach, which was Jen's idea, would minimize the number of days employees were off and the doors were closed. He wasn't sure how to tell anyone, yet. Not that he imagined too many of them would have a problem with staying home and collecting paychecks, but people could be funny. That was the biggest thing he'd learned from working in the hospitality industry.

"Hey." Andie joined him behind the counter. "Any word on Marlon?"

"Yep. I talked to Jacob a few hours ago. They released him."

"No. That's terrible. Do you think he'll show up at the farm for the engagement party?"

Chad shrugged. "If he does, security will recognize him and stop him before he reaches the supply building. If he somehow gets past them, Jacob will be there. Off-duty or not, he'll step in."

Andie wedged herself between the counter and him. He didn't like the infringement on his personal space, but he held his ground rather than make a scene.

"It should be a nice night." She was fishing.

He looked over her head at the crowded restaurant for a reason to escape. "I'm sure it will be. Zoe's in charge."

"Do you have a date?"

"Andie … "

"It's an innocent question."

But his answer wouldn't be. Not to her. Not after all the conversations about how dating an employee went against his principles. She was already asking too many questions about why Jen was in town for the weekend, and her persistent chatter about him not answering his phone last night had worn him thin.

He raised the cup to his lips to stifle any incriminating words. A manager didn't owe his employees details about his personal life, especially when those details were … sticky.

Monica, the waitress least likely to give him any guff, walked behind the counter with a check in hand. "Are we having a juicy gossip sesh?"

She hip checked Chad away from the front of the register and punched the keyboard until the drawer released.

Andie huffed and walked away.

"Ooh, sorry I asked."

He knew better than to fan the fire by saying something about Andie's mood, but sometimes saying nothing was worse. "After last night, we're all a little testy."

Monica nodded.

He stood there, clutching his coffee, staring out the window at the two-lane street. If he were home, he'd grab Jen by the hand and walk aimlessly down the dirt road, enjoying the peace. Maybe she was doing that now—without him—because she was bored. He frowned.

How was leaving her alone in a strange place helping him convince her to give them a chance?

• • •

"I could drive you," Jen said. She wasn't the kind of person to get involved, let alone offer to chauffeur a virtual stranger twenty minutes away to pick up some baked goods, but this weekend was turning out to be a lesson in living outside her comfort zone, so why not?

"Are you sure?" Zoe's eyes were bluer than anything Jen had ever seen. She was pert and polished, and Jen was convinced she'd been fed misinformation.

There was no way in hell a woman like that shared DNA with a man who charged into restaurants drunk and ended up in the slammer.

Jen nodded. "I've got nothing better to do."

Noon had come and gone without another word from Chad. Apparently, he was busy. And now, she was busy, too. That helped to dull her uncertainty over being here. "Excellent." Zoe clapped. Literally.

Jen smirked. There really was no way in hell.

"I'll call Courtney and let her know she doesn't have to turn around. That way she can unload what's in my car and start getting things set up so we won't waste time."

Patty and a pretty woman named Ashley, who was somehow related to Chad, strung white lights from wood beams on the far side of the room. Jen wouldn't call her overall feeling comfortable in the company of perfect strangers, but she wasn't sweating buckets over being here, either. Resignation was the name of the game—at least until she saw Chad again and knew where she stood.

She was fully prepared to walk away if he told he was having second thoughts about being with her beyond the brew pub pitch. Really.

"Okay. Let's go." Zoe called out a chipper goodbye to the women at the back and then headed for the door.

It took the entire twenty-minute drive to get through Adam and Zoe's romantic history, which wasn't exactly surprising, considering it spanned more than a decade. Also, Zoe liked to talk. Amazingly, Jen didn't mind listening. It was better than overthinking.

As she walked around the bakery showroom, she admired the crisp white shelves and too-pretty-to-eat treats. A bakery suited Zoe like Jen imagined a brewery suited her.

"This one and this one." Zoe was breathless as she lifted stacked plastic containers onto a marble countertop.

Jen rushed forward. "Let me help."

Zoe pushed a clump of dark hair off her face. "Thanks, but I'm a little bit of a control freak. It's still a novelty to have people around me to help. I don't know. Maybe it always will be." She smiled, but then her smile faded. "I'm sure you heard about my dad."

Jen nodded. A sliver of regret for being curious about the information stuck in her heart. She recognized the embarrassment lining Zoe's face. Gossip hurt. Gossip because of something your parents did sucked the life right out of you.

"I heard," she said. "I was with Chad when he got the call."

Zoe ripped a sticky note off a pad and scribbled something before she pressed the paper to the plastic container. "You know, I used to think I could save him—get him clean, or whatever you want to call it. But it's too much for one person. Apparently, it's too much for a whole town." She sighed. "Still, I feel like I'm the bad guy keeping him away tonight."

"You're not." Jen shook her head a little too emphatically, enough to feel her brain rattle against her skull. Nobody knew the strain of trying to keep a parent away like she did. "My parents are no model citizens, either. We do what we have to do to survive. Just remember, they don't define us."

The words didn't even feel like hers. They were nothing she'd ever thought before. Who knew where they came from? As long as they helped Zoe.

If only Jen could believe they applied to her situation, too.

Zoe stared at her for the longest time, the sweetest smile on her face. "Thanks." She reached out, squeezed Jen's hand, and then slid the top plastic container toward her. "You can carry this one, but keep it level. Cupcakes are precious cargo."

Jen laughed, if for no other reason than Zoe Miller was proof good people could come from lousy parents.

Chapter Eleven

Chad walked into the supply building, which had seen its fair share of transformations. Once a bare bones, utilitarian space, his cousin, Ashley, had turned it into a tea showplace complete with artwork, mood lighting, tasting counters, and surround sound music to lull vendors into submission. But he'd never seen it like this—strung with tiny white lights, sparkling with silver ribbon. It was like something out of a magazine for hopeless romantics.

He took a deep breath, sucking in the familiar, earthy scent of tea stored in close proximity, and scanned the buzzing room for Jen. He liked that she had a hand in this. He just hoped she wasn't ready to strangle him for leaving her alone with them. His family could be over-the-top enthusiastic and a bit smothering.

He couldn't imagine Jen enjoying those traits.

A flash of dark hair caught his eye across the room. She was on the lowest rung of a ladder being steadied by Patty. No pink boots this time, but a similar pair of hip-hugging jeans accentuated her frame. Lust slammed him hard in the gut.

He hated that it took him so long to get to her.

Walking, he smiled and said "hello" to everyone he passed, but he never really took his eyes off Jen.

"Chad, thank God." Patty rushed him. "We need somebody tall to hang the other end of this banner. Jen almost fell on her third attempt."

Behind her, Jen hopped to the floor, an expression he couldn't read on her face. Either she was annoyed at her lack of banner-hanging success, or she wasn't particularly happy to see him. His smile faltered on the last thought.

"Sure." He looked at the banner in question and then back at Jen, who stood off to the side of the ladder. "Sorry it took me so long."

Jen glanced at Patty and then back at him, her gaze softening and a small grin tipping her lips. "You said that already in your text."

He did, but it deserved repeating, especially now that it resulted in a break in her unreadable mood.

"This needs to be hooked up there." Patty held the corner of the banner via her finger through a brass loop.

He wished Jen had been waiting for him at home where they could talk and settle a few things without everyone hovering. But she was here, so he took the banner from Patty and climbed the ladder to complete the task.

In the end, it was worth it. He felt Jen's eyes on him the entire time. Twice he glanced over his shoulder and caught her staring. The blush on her face didn't seem compatible with concern for his safety.

Maybe she was remembering the last time one of them was on a ladder … and how they ended up wrapped in each other's arms. He was, and those memories produced the best feeling he'd had all day.

Back on the ground, he sidled up to her, determined to get her alone. "Do you think you can get away?"

She opened that beautiful mouth and managed, "I … "

"Jen, does this look like it will work?"

He stifled a groan of frustration and turned toward Zoe's voice. She was holding up a black chord with a silver tip.

"Not yet," Jen whispered to him as she brushed past.

He watched the women congregate, huddled over the wire. What the heck? He thought he'd abandoned her for half the day and worried she'd be inundated with a million reasons why she wanted to be anyplace but here when all along, she'd been making friends and carrying on fine without him.

Pride was a funny thing. It came out of nowhere, puffing his chest and plastering a smile on his face. He was proud of her. There was a lot he didn't know about her, but he knew it couldn't have been easy to jump right in and spend the day with a bunch of strangers. Heck, the first night they'd met, she'd been prepared to do God only knew what with him without divulging much more than her first name. Sociability didn't seem to rank high on her list of amusements. And yet, here she was being more than social—she was being helpful, too.

She amazed him time and time again. Beauty, brains, boldness, strength, and now she was laughing with Zoe like they were old friends.

He added adaptability to the list.

"Can I help?" he asked, giving in to the vicious need to be a part of anything that included her.

Just standing next to her feeling the subtle heat radiating from her body had him buzzing.

"That's okay. Jen knows amps." Zoe gave a little hop and squeal. "Thank you so, so much." And then she was gone.

He grinned through his confusion. "You know amps?"

Jen's eyes sparkled up at him, and she added a self-deprecating shrug. "I do. Mara's a singer. I've been her roadie a time or two."

"Of course you have." He chuckled, envisioning her hunched over band equipment in a T-shirt and jeans, her dark hair shimmering in the stage lights.

The laughter caught on a lump in his throat.

"What?" Her bold brows furrowed.

He tossed his arm around her shoulder and tucked her against him, getting a full-on blast of spice from her hair. It stirred the flames lapping at his core.

"You just surprise me."

Somehow he managed to keep his lips off her as they walked through the busy room. He still wasn't sure how Dad would take the news that Chad had so suddenly progressed to something more than business with Jen.

"Is it a good thing that I surprise you?" she asked.

"Yeah, it's good. Why wouldn't it be good?"

"I don't like surprises."

Something told him he needed to remember that.

• • •

Jen stood in the middle of the big bedroom, staring at herself in a full-length mirror. The black mini-dress she had worn beneath her college graduation gown looked brand new, probably because she hadn't worn it since. Dressing up wasn't really her thing.

She ran a finger over the velvet crisscrossing her breasts, showing just enough skin to make her feel sexy without being self-conscious. If the skirt had been tight instead of pleated, she could've added that to her list of worries. As it was, the list wasn't nearly as long as she expected it to be.

After spending the afternoon decorating the supply building and getting to know Chad's family, she felt useful. She'd made friends. It was a pseudo-sense of belonging.

She didn't expect anyone to question why she was there anymore. Besides, they already had their ideas. The microbrewery was on everyone's lips, and a few times Zoe even referred to Chad and Jen in a couples capacity. Considering he couldn't keep his hands off her while they were decorating, that made sense.

Jen didn't know how to feel about the rapid change in their relationship. She flattened a sweaty palm to her midsection. Did two make-out sessions and a bunch of business lunches and dinners qualify anyone for couplehood?

Maybe a couple-of-morons-hood.

She spun toward the bed on a wave of fresh doubt. The surges came and went every few hours, leaving her wondering when a high tide would completely take her out.

Chills picked at her skin, and she fished in her suitcase for the shawl Mara reminded her to pack. Sleeveless was tricky in these parts. Temperatures could plummet at night, and what if it rained?

Sheer curtains rippled in the evening breeze, compounding Jen's nerve-wracking anticipation. This night held so much promise—too much. What if she flaked out like she always did when someone was interested in more than sex with her?

With Patty gone into town to prepare for the evening, the house was eerily quiet. But these walls could probably tell a few tales—happy ones. Good things could come from relationships. Closing her eyes, she pictured a family, heard the low rumble of a man calling out to his wife ... kids laughing ... puppies barking ... the lawnmower whirring ... the motor buzzing and buzzing until ...

Shit. That was her phone.

She grabbed the black box beside the suitcase. *Blocked call.* Either a job or Mom. One would leave a message. The other she didn't want to deal with right now.

Jen let the call go to voicemail.

Seconds later, the phone vibrated in her hand, but not with the voicemail she expected. Instead, a text message lit the screen.

It's me on Mick's phone. Your mom's in town. I told her you were away.

Jen dropped to the edge of the bed. Years of embarrassment clogged her throat. Mom was in Seattle, not in Emerald Springs, but the need to hide raged inside of Jen until she was squeezing her phone so tightly the plastic case made an ominous cracking sound.

What if Mom figured out where she was? What if she came to Emerald Springs looking for her? Richard Whitman was wealthy and unmarried. Gloria Chavez would have a field day here.

Don't talk to her again. Don't tell her anything.

Jen typed with shaky fingers.

Her heart hammered in her ears as she hit send. Surely she was overreacting.

"Hey."

Chad. She heard the steps creak beneath his weight.

"Are you decent?" He laughed.

God, she wished she could laugh with him.

"Up here," she called, alarmed by the raw sound of her voice.

The door swung open. Concern knitted his brow. "You okay?"

He already knew she wasn't, and that sucked. She'd always been so careful to protect herself from vulnerabilities. It sucked even more that she couldn't dwell on his gorgeous body wrapped in a black-on-black suit.

"What's going on?" He came to her, dropping to his knees. One hand rested on the mattress beside her, the other slid to her waist.

She stared at her bare knees. "Just …"

Her phone vibrated again, the screen on full display. She should hide it from him. But he'd only ask her to explain.

"My mother surprised me with a visit." The words left a sting in her throat. After this conversation was through, Chad would be through with her, too. "I should go." She stood, forcing him to stand.

"Wait." With a hook of his finger he lifted her chin, forcing eye contact. "I couldn't help but read the texts. What's going on?"

She found a tiny spot of peeling wallpaper to anchor her watery gaze. "Just let me go. You're going to want me to go."

"Jen … " He kissed her forehead, the warmth from his soft lips seeping into her aching head.

She managed a shaky breath, bolstered by the kiss and the knowledge that the Whitmans knew all about Zoe's mess, yet they let her marry into the family. Surely, they wouldn't hold Jen's mess against her. After all, the only proposal she'd received was to brew their beer.

"My mom is … troubled." Her tongue didn't cooperate. It felt fat and clumsy, and the words didn't form. She wished someone would tell the story for her.

"Like mentally ill?"

God, Jen dropped her head to his chest and actually laughed— not a good laugh, one brought on by a childhood spent scared to death, always wondering what the hell was wrong and when it was going to get her, too.

Chad smoothed her hair, kissed the top of her head, and she wanted time to freeze. If she could stay here—caught in this in-between—she'd be happy.

"No. I mean, I don't think so. I don't know." She rocked her head back and forth against the crisp-smelling cloth, letting his citrus and spice scent soothe her.

Funny how she could be broken, and okay, all in one emotional moment.

"Is she dangerous?" He dropped his hand to the bare skin above her zipper and held her close.

Jen shook her head. "Only in a manipulative way." The words flowed on the strength of his hand against her back. Somehow this man she'd met at one of the lowest moments in her life made her want to risk telling him the truth. "She lies, cheats, steals, sells her body, sells her soul." Her chest convulsed. "And for most of my life, she said she did it to provide for me because my dad left … and he left because of me."

More convulsions, deeper convulsions, but no real sound, just the strange intake of air that never made it where it was needed most. Her heart.

"Hey." He took her hand, led her to the bed, and settled them both in the space beside the open suitcase. "Look at me."

She really didn't want to. This was the most pathetic thing she'd ever done, breaking down like this. How could he look at her and see anything but what she really was? Chaos in his perfect world.

He took control, lifting her chin again. This time, he held her face in his hands, holding her up for his scrutiny.

Everything hurt, ached. Her lungs screamed from lack of air. Her stomach muscles burned from the violent heaves. And her head folded beneath the pressure. She closed her eyes rather than look at his crinkled face.

The brush of his lips against her mouth startled her, and she parted her lips. His tongue, soft and wet, traced a gentle path along the seam, demanding nothing in return, offering the sweetest distraction from the pain.

Ridding her hands of the phone, she curled her fingers into his lapel and pulled him closer.

His hands warmed her cheeks. His thumbs strummed her jaw. *This* somehow fixed everything.

She opened her mouth wider and touched her tongue to his.

He kissed her hot and hard and deep, drawing her closer, holding her tighter, but letting her go too soon.

Breathing heavily, he studied her. "None of what your parents did was because of you."

He was still holding her face, but softer now. His fingers traced the length of her throat, and she welcomed the easier swallows. If only her heart rate would settle, then maybe she could breathe without the embarrassing hitch.

"You're not responsible for them."

Maybe not, but they were responsible for her. Didn't that say something?

"I don't expect you to understand," she said. Chad's DNA was from a respectable man like Richard Whitman. She could only image how wonderful his mother had been.

"I'd like to."

Such a good guy. Why would he want to be saddled with her? She wiggled free of his hands.

"Talk to me, Jen." The concern on his face multiplied her guilt.

They were supposed to be at his brother's engagement party, not wallowing in her miserable lineage, and she'd had enough of it. She wouldn't wallow anymore.

"What are you afraid of?" He pushed.

He deserved the truth. "That I'm just like them. That I'll lie and cheat and steal and leave if I'm given the chance."

The concern faded from his face, and something steely lit his eyes. When his cheek pulsed, any composure she'd gained crumbled beneath her.

He knew it was true. If she stayed, she was going to hurt him.

She needed to go.

Chapter Twelve

Chad just needed a minute to compartmentalize things.

Jen wasn't Tasha. This wasn't the same thing. But the words *lie, cheat,* and *steal* wrapped around his sensible thoughts and knotted everything together in his head.

She was upset and scared, and he was a jerk for allowing this sliver of doubt to get in their way.

You don't know her, came the escalating, responsible voice in his head.

And yet he knew she liked ketchup and mustard with her fries, refused to listen to anything but indie rock on the radio, and tackled everything—including him—with a healthy dose of skepticism.

He supposed he knew her, and he didn't. This revelation about her family was proof. But what did it really matter?

There were things about him she didn't know, too. That didn't make him a bad guy. That didn't make this a bad idea. It just meant they had more to learn.

"I'm going to go. It's okay." She stood.

He hadn't even had a chance to tell her how amazing she looked, draped in elegant black, her hair hanging loose. Her face was splotchy and puffy with pent-up emotion, and she was the most beautiful thing on earth.

"Stay." He took her hand, pressed it to his lips, and didn't let the thought of more revelations or her sober expression chase him away.

There was too much to lose.

Somehow he would lighten the mood and get things back on track. "I'm not going to my brother's engagement party alone. Can you imagine how bad that would look? I'm supposed to be a lady's man."

Her veneer didn't crack. Instead, she released a patronizing sigh. "What are we doing, Chad?" She stood there, shaking her head, looking down at him sitting on the edge of the bed like he was a fool. "Why are we acting like this?"

"Like what?" A jolt of anger tightened his jaw. He never did like being questioned.

"Like we're something more than two people who pulled off funding for a microbrewery, and even that was jacked. You're rich. Your father wasn't going to turn you down. God, he worships you. They all do. All you needed to do was wake up and claim what's been yours all along. Maybe you needed me to help you see that, but you don't need me now."

He growled, using the force of the sound to stand until he was in her face, breath for breath. "If it's true, then why do I want you so badly?"

She lowered her gaze, resignation in her drooping shoulders. "I don't know."

He did. Microbrewery or not, they were meant to see this through.

"Tell me you don't want me," he said.

"I … can't."

He cupped her face in his hands like he'd done before and drew her lips to his mouth. Just a taste because anything more would guarantee they'd never leave this house.

"We're going to the party. We're going to enjoy ourselves, and then you're coming home with me."

And this time, nothing was going to get in his way.

• • •

Jen held onto Chad's arm as they walked into the crowded room. It felt different than it had that afternoon while she was part of the small decorating crew. The twinkling lights, the buzz of conversation, and the bombardment of sugary and spicy smells overwhelmed her now. Maybe that was because after what happened at the house, she was as raw as she'd ever been.

And amazingly, after seeing her fall apart, Chad still wanted her to stay.

He'd guided her out of the house with his arm around her waist. He'd held her hand on the drive over, and now this—arms locked like he was afraid if he let her go, she would run.

She didn't feel like running anymore.

"Are you sure you're not my sister? You're too pretty to be a boy."

The voice came from behind them, and Jen turned at Chad's subtle tug.

"Hey, man," Chad said, grabbing onto the impeccably groomed man's hand, and bringing him in for a shoulder bump.

He never let go of Jen.

"Dan, this is Jen. Jen, this is my brother Daniel."

The men separated, and Daniel flashed a brilliant smile. "Ah! The brewmistress extraordinaire." He presented his hand to her palm up, all suave and debonair. "It's nice to finally meet you."

She slipped her hand onto his and waited for whatever came next.

It was an odd sort of handshake, gentle and flirtatious, even. She could only smile. "It's nice to meet you, too."

Chad pushed their hands apart. "Enough. Find your own woman," he said laughing.

"I'll pass," Daniel said with an eye roll. "But I will find myself another drink." He looked beyond them, and his face tensed. Apparently he saw something he didn't like, but Chad was holding Jen too tightly for her to manage anything more than an eyeful of his wide chest.

Not that she was complaining. After losing it on that chest an hour ago, she had a newfound appreciation for it.

"We'll talk," Chad said.

"Yeah, we will," Daniel answered.

It was all very cryptic.

When Daniel had walked away, Jen glanced up at Chad. "Is everything okay?"

He nodded. "It will be."

She followed his line of sight to the far side of the room where Mr. Whitman and Patty stood in a group that included Adam and Zoe. Pretty people were everywhere. She had no idea what the problem was. Her gaze locked on Zoe, smiling as she looked up at Adam. Backlit by sparkling lights, wearing a pale yellow dress, she was almost glowing.

"Is it … " Jen whispered to Chad, "Zoe's dad?"

"What? No." He shook his head, and some of the puzzlement left his face. "It's … " he dropped his mouth to her ear, causing a delicious shudder, "Patty and my dad. Dan's just loyal."

When he pulled back and looked her in the eyes, her mind went black. She could smell his cinnamon breath and feel the heat from his beautiful body—what else mattered? Only that he wanted her here. He knew the truth about her, and still he asked her to stay.

She'd never been so wholly accepted by anyone other than Mara.

"We should say 'hello.'" He was smiling, the expression crinkling the skin around his golden eyes.

"We should." She smiled back.

And he kissed her right there. Not a hot, attention-grabbing kiss. Just a quick, sweet nip.

Her toes curled anyway.

As they crossed the room, he shifted his arm to the hollow of her waist, holding her against him. It was the most wonderful place she'd ever been. No roof over her head, no lock on her door ever made her feel this safe.

His family smiled and urged them closer. Warmth unrelated to his touch flushed her throat and face. No family of hers ever made her feel this loved.

But then what did she know about love?

Zoe squealed and hugged Jen—first, before she hugged her future brother-in-law. How cool was that? Her sense of belonging deepened. Then there were more hugs from Patty and Adam. Even Richard, who eyed them intently, leaned in for a hug.

Jen was swallowing hyperactively now, blinking against a burning in her eyes as conversation erupted.

Richard looked once at Chad's arm around her waist, but went on with his conversation like nothing was out of the ordinary.

How could she possibly fight something that was happening so effortlessly? For some reason, against all odds, they fit—she fit.

And she was ready to be a part of this for as long as they would have her.

•••

Chad pulled Jen onto the makeshift dance floor amid strains of Eric Clapton. He'd always loved this song, and it seemed appropriate to share it with her. She looked him deep in the eyes a second before she settled her head over his heart. Threading fingers through her hair, he leaned his cheek against her forehead.

Tonight may have started out rocky, but it was turning out better than he could've dreamed, especially after he managed a brief conversation with Dad about everything that had happened in the last twenty-four hours. Maybe it was the party atmosphere, but Dad didn't seem overly concerned about Marlon causing a ruckus at the diner last night, or Chad's deepening relationship with Jen. Then again, maybe it was because Dad had more to worry about after Daniel's less-than-thrilled reaction to seeing him with Patty.

Whatever the reason for the heat to be deflected off Chad, he was grateful. And he was happy. Right here, on the dance floor with Jen, where they barely moved. They simply swayed. He could've stayed like this forever.

Maybe he was falling in love with her. Maybe this outrageous feeling of contentment was the start of what his parents had. Attraction, admiration, friendship, respect. He'd never felt all of those things at once for anyone else.

She looked at him. "Would you really want me to be your brewmaster?"

He slid a palm to her cheek and brushed his thumb over the pad of her bottom lip. From the beating of his heart to his inhales and exhales, everything was slow and steady. "More than anything." Which wasn't exactly true because right here, right now, he wanted her looking up at him like this forever more than anything else.

"Okay." Her smiled was shaky. "Then I will."

The words exploded in his chest, scattering joy throughout his body. He squeezed her to him, resting his chin on her head. With his eyes shut, he let the happiness soak in.

This was their beginning. He didn't need to worry about another job taking her away.

He opened his eyes and the smile fell from his face.

Andie was standing on the far side of the room, shooting daggers.

Well, hell. So much for no worries.

* * *

"Hey, Boss."

The woman from the diner didn't acknowledge Jen, so Jen ignored her, too, smiling at the large man beside her.

For the first time all evening, Chad let her go.

"Andie. Jacob." He nodded and shook the man's hand. "I'm surprised to see you here … together."

Jen stole a glance at Andie, who was looking rather smug.

"It was a last minute thing, right Jake?"

Jacob straightened until he looked downright stiff.

What an odd couple.

"I wasn't sure I was going to make it," Jacob said, shifting his gaze around the room.

"I'm glad you did," Chad said, keeping his eyes on the man. "I want you to meet someone. This is Jen Chavez. She's a brewmaster from Seattle. Jen, this is my good friend, Jacob Sanders. He's the long arm of the law around here."

Jacob grinned. "Nice to meet you, Jen."

Andie's nose wrinkled like the snout of a great white shark. "You two were cute and cozy out there on the dance floor."

Chad ignored her. "Any word on Marlon?"

"Nope," Jacob said. "It's all quiet."

"Good. Let's hope it stays that way." Chad smacked the man on the upper arm. "I'll catch you later." He tossed a quick, half smile at Andie. "Now if you'll excuse us … "

He led Jen away.

"What was that?" she asked as they disappeared into the crowd.

"My cue that I need to start looking for a new assistant manager."

It didn't make sense.

Ashley stepped into their path, her pretty face twisted. "Why is *he* here?"

Jen's mind reeled.

"Ash, chill. He's been my friend almost as long as you've been my cousin. Besides, he can keep things under control if Marlon shows up."

Ashley sneered at Chad. "What if he has … " she eyed up Jen, like she wasn't sure she should be saying anything in front of her, "ulterior motives?"

It was downright uncomfortable—it had been for a few minutes now. *Genetic Molotov cocktails.* She excused herself to the ladies room. It would give Chad and his cousin some time to hash out whatever family drama needed tending to.

Two steps down the hall and a few feet from the swinging door, Jen felt a tap on her should.

"I like your dress." Andie smiled, but it wasn't friendly.

The toothy grin made Jen's arm hair stand on end. "Thanks."

Andie followed her into the ladies room. Jen prayed for crowded conditions.

Unfortunately, the room was empty—perfect for conversation. She bolted for the nearest stall.

Andie filed into the stall beside her.

Talk about uncomfortable.

"So you and Chad are a couple? That's so awesome."

There was a harsh tone to her words.

Jen stood in the stall, debating her answer and next move. She felt trapped.

"It's nice to see he's gotten past the whole Tasha thing. She nearly destroyed him and his family."

The toilet flushed, the whooshing sound in eerie harmony with the sound of her brain whirling for a reaction to the cryptic announcement. How long could she go without answering? Could she outlast Andie by staying in the stall?

Strappy black sandals appeared at the gap along the bottom of Jen's door. "He always said he'd never date an employee again. You must be *very special.*"

The last two words made Jen's skin crawl. She spun around and hit the toilet handle with the ball of her foot, hoping the loud noise would somehow chase Andie away.

It didn't.

Resigned to facing the venomous woman, Jen lifted her chin and unlatched the door.

Andie stepped back with a shitty grin on her face. "Enjoy your night."

And then she was gone.

Jen stared at the swinging door. Half of her wanted to go after the woman and even the score, but the other half urged her to take the advice for what it was worth.

Enjoy your night. Jen could handle that.

She recognized a jealous woman when she saw one—another oddly helpful thing she learned from her mother. Whatever Andie hoped to accomplish with her little performance had backfired.

Turning toward the mirror, Jen adjusted her dress, revealing an inch more cleavage. She fluffed her skirt, ran fingers through her hair, and then left the ladies room.

She had one thing on her mind: convincing Chad it was time to go home.

Chapter Thirteen

Chad leaned against the tasting-counter-turned-bar. He sipped the craft beer he'd stashed behind the counter while they'd decorated that afternoon and waited for Jen.

What a night. Between Jen's emotional revelation about her mother, Dan's reaction to seeing Dad and Patty together, Andie's reaction to seeing Chad with Jen, and Ashley's reaction to seeing Jacob, he was partied out. He wanted nothing more than to go home and shut out the rest of the world so he could have …

That.

Jen walked toward him through a gap in the crowd. She wore a crooked smile on her determined face. There was sass in her hip swing and plenty of sun-kissed skin to admire as her breasts overflowed the crisscrossed neckline of her dress.

He set the bottle on the counter and stepped to her like metal to a magnet.

She gave her head a little shake and tossed her hair over her shoulder. "I'm ready when you are."

The innocent words had a not-so-innocent impact on his body. With his pulse heavy and his groin hard, his gaze dropped from her lips to her bulging breasts. "Ready for what?" he teased.

"Whatever you have in mind."

Hell. He didn't have anything in mind because his temperature had skyrocketed enough to burn brain cells.

Thank God his body knew what to do. He grabbed her hand and led her to the door.

"Should we say good night?"

"Good night," he called over his shoulder to no one and everyone at the same time.

She giggled, and he felt invincible. Talk about a rush.

Outside in the darkness sensation overruled. Warmth from their joined hands traveled the length of his arm, priming his body. And even though he was in excellent shape, he was breathless by the time he reached the Jeep.

As he held the passenger side door open, Jen climbed in, careful not to catch her heel. He smelled her so vividly, he could taste her on his tongue. Guided by the dome light, she pulled her legs into the car, and he touched her knee like he had in the parking lot of the brewery supply store. Only this time, he gave himself permission to linger, to toy with the subtle curve of her inner thigh, and to grin when she sighed and wrapped a hand around his wrist, pressing her fingernails into his skin.

Leaning in, he kissed her, joining their warm lips for a couple of breaths. And then he opened her mouth with a nudge of his tongue and slipped inside.

She grabbed the back of his head with the same urgency she grabbed his wrist.

He moved his hand beneath her dress and used his thumb to stroke a line atop her satin panties.

Her moan caught in his mouth as she pressed her bottom half against his hand.

He was hot and hard, and seconds away from … making a scene in the parking lot of his brother's engagement party.

"Hey," he whispered against her wet lips. "Let's … "

"Get out of here." She released her grip on his neck and wrist.

He smiled the whole way around to the driver's side door, despite the awkward hitch in his step and the ache in his groin.

Jen was quiet as he maneuvered the vehicle out of its spot and onto the dimly lit rocky road. Two miles back to his place was a long time to stay quiet, but he wasn't sure what to say. He didn't want to talk. He wanted to run his tongue over every inch of her body and then bury himself inside of her, which probably wasn't the thing to say if he wanted this drive home to be anywhere near comfortable. He squirmed against the pressure in his pants. Maybe mundane conversation would come to him once the blood returned to the head on his shoulders.

Or not …

Her hand slid over his thigh and straight to his erection. *Bold.* He liked it.

She rubbed him, saying nothing, looking straight ahead. It was a dangerous game.

He ground his teeth to keep from succumbing to the pressure. "Jen … "

"Relax," she whispered. "Go slow."

Easy for her to say.

And then she had him in her hands, her body folding over the center console so she could reach him with her mouth.

Pulling over on the side of the dark road, he dropped his head to the seat behind him, threaded his fingers through her hair, and let her consume him.

No thoughts. No words. No sounds. Just sensation after sensation until orgasm ripped a guttural moan from his throat.

All of him went limp at her command.

When she'd fastened him back up and placed a sweet kiss at the base of his neck, he wrapped her in his arms.

"Thank you," he whispered into the cushion of her hair.

"Welcome," she returned, winding her arms around his middle.

Quiet ensued. A simple peace.

He closed his eyes, hypnotized by her warm weight and his gentle breathing.

He didn't know love aside from the family kind, but he wanted it to be this, and he wanted it to be her.

Now that she was staying he had all the time in the world to make sure it happened.

• • •

There was something supremely satisfying about taking a man from the brink of chaos to the point of peace. But now that they were in a room with a bed, peaceful was the last word Jen would use to describe Chad.

He shrugged out of his suit coat without taking his eyes off of her, his expression dark and determined. He tugged the shirttails from his pants. With one hand to her waist, he pulled her against him, crushing her lips with his.

They'd been here before: joined at the mouth, on the edge of something bigger. He dragged her zipper down to her lower back, sliding a warm hand across her sensitive skin, and then he slipped his tongue into her mouth. Sweet surrender. She let the dress fall to her feet.

He traced the curves of her ass with his palms and stroked feather-light along the skin of her waist, causing goose pimples over her body. She couldn't breathe fast enough to keep up with her heartbeat, and it was a delicious rush.

Then he was at her breasts, guiding them from the black lace, warming them in his hands.

Her nipples hardened beneath his palms, and she lifted her chin so he could plant kisses on her neck, swallowing against the glorious pressure of his mouth.

"I want to make this work—us work." His words were raspy, spoken inches from her heart.

"Me, too." They were the right words to say, even if she didn't know what to do to make any of it true.

He lifted her, carried her to the bed, and settled them both on the mattress. There'd been times in her life when she'd felt strong, capable, and able to survive completely on her own. She thought happiness was tied to that independence. And yet here, vulnerable, confused, and at his mercy, she'd never been happier.

Undressing felt like stripping back the layers between them, until there was nothing left. They were skin-to-skin, mouth-to-mouth. Bared.

Chad's hand roamed her body, tickling and teasing. She wiggled toward him, hitching a leg over his hip, seeking his center. She found his fingers instead, probing, playing, and tipping her sanity to the breaking point.

Jen gripped his shoulders as she rode the wave, his mouth quieting her moans. And when orgasm rocked her body, its power left her shattered.

"Chad," she gasped against his warm chest.

He held her close, kissed her neck, his erection pressing against her thigh. Step by step they were coming closer to something she'd never overthought before.

Sex. It was a short word, a harsh word, but this was more. Maybe it was post-orgasmic romanticizing. She would've given that more credence if this had been her first orgasm. But it wasn't.

She'd never felt like this.

Opening her eyes, Jen palmed his face. Foreign words formed on her tongue. *Love.* It roared through her mind like a runaway train. No. She loved *this*, not *him*. It was too soon for it to be the other way around, too complicated, too … perfect. He made her feel like *she* was perfect, like when they were together anything was possible.

He brushed fingers over her taunt nipples as he smiled down at her. "You're the most beautiful woman in the world."

She chuckled. "You're not bad yourself."

And then he rolled her onto her back until he covered her.

She widened her legs, letting him settle between her thighs, welcoming the warmth and peace with her mouth on his neck and her hands on his ass.

"You still ready for whatever I have in mind?" he asked.

She grinned. "I was ready the night we met."

The question was, was she ready for this?

• • •

With a condom in place, Chad pushed inside of her, holding steady while her body cradled him. It felt too good to move, but not moving seemed weird, so he pulled out and pushed back in, squeezing his eyes as tightly as the rest of his muscles, as tightly as her arms and legs wrapped around him.

Her lips were on his neck, her tongue tracing circles on his Adam's apple.

"Harder," she moaned.

He surged and obliged, dropping his mouth to her breast, somehow keeping pace with their lower halves.

"Yes."

It was a mutual affirmation. They panted and burned, pushed and pulled, until he growled in her ear and surrendered.

With one more press inside her, she shuddered beneath him.

He rolled them to their sides, burying his face in the crook of her neck, cushioned by her body, too joyous and satisfied to speak.

She sighed, creating a little rumble in her throat. "I like you."

He smiled because coming from Jen, those were some heavy words.

Hours later, a little after two, Chad slipped out of bed to use the bathroom. Upon his return, he lingered in the doorway, watching her sleep. She curled on her side, facing his pillow, her chin tipping toward a swath of moonlight.

She was his future.

He could see days spanning out before them. Jen in her pink boots, smiling at him from behind the brew house glass. Stolen kisses behind his office door. And nights like this, watching her sleep after they made love.

There it was again. That word. *Love.*

He wasn't sure he bought into the fairy tale version of romance and soul mates, or some magic event that appeared out of the blue. Instead, he saw love as a choice, a calculated decision, an *I choose you*, followed by a solemn vow to do whatever it took to make it last a lifetime.

That seemed plausible. *That* seemed doable.

With his eyes on Jen, Chad crawled back into bed and snuggled against her.

"I choose you," he whispered into the darkness.

She made a happy sound against his chest as she stirred. "What?" Her voice was heavy with sleep.

"I choose you."

"For what?"

"For everything."

She cuddled closer on a sigh. "That's so nice."

He smiled because it was—nicer than he ever dreamed it would be.

As he drifted in and out of sleep, an endless string of days, months, and years unfolded. The monotony had always scared him. But not anymore. He'd found his way, his place in his family, and the woman he wanted by his side every day.

In this moment, he had no doubt Mom would've been proud.

• • •

Brightness woke Jen from a sound sleep. *Sunshine.* But then she opened her eyes and saw the dark room divided by the hallway light.

Chad was missing from bed, but she could hear the low rumble of his voice in the other room.

The clock read 3:13 A.M. She sat, wrapped a quilt around her naked body, and went to find him.

"I'll be right there," he said.

Based on the last time he rushed out on her, she jumped to the same conclusion. Zoe's dad was at it again.

Chad met her in the hallway. He was shirtless, wearing open-fly jeans. Under any other circumstance, she would've ogled, but his glum expression told her the admiration would be out of place.

"What happened?" she asked.

"That was the security company. The fire alarm at the diner is going off." He pushed past her. "Hopefully it's a false alarm. It happens sometimes."

She watched him dress, noting the deep lines carving his face. His movements were forceful and sharp.

"Go back to sleep," he said.

"I can't, not until I know you're okay."

He came to her, wrapped her in his arms, and kissed her forehead. "Hurry up. Get dressed. You can come with me. All I have to do is meet the fire department and make sure the coast is clear. With any luck, we'll be back in bed before sunrise."

Two hours later, Jen was staring bleary-eyed at a cup of coffee while sitting on a stool in Zoe's bakery.

"My father has done a lot of terrible things, but I can't imagine him starting a fire at the diner." Zoe stacked freshly baked muffins on a crystal cake plate, readying for the morning rush.

Jen didn't know what to say. She didn't know what to think, either. All she knew was that Chad was at the diner where a fire in the backroom had caused considerable damage. Fortunately, it wasn't a total loss, but how would this impact him, her, and the microbrewery?

"Did they say if there were any signs of forced entry?"

Jen shook her head. "Not while I was there."

By now they should know more, and by now she had hoped to hear from Chad. The lack of communication made her antsy.

"Maybe it was an accident. Just a fluke."

"Maybe."

But Jen couldn't shake the feeling of foreboding. It hounded her like the sleep she was missing. In her exhaustion, all she could see was her final confrontation with Andie.

"How well do you know Andie from the diner?" she asked.

Zoe placed the crystal lid on the cake plate and blinked at Jen. "I don't really. What I know of her is secondhand. She dated Chad a couple of times, but then she needed a job so he hired her instead. Why?"

Jen stared at the black, steaming liquid in her cup. Knowing Andie had dated Chad before she went to work for him clarified the little tirade in the ladies room. "She said some things to me last night, and after this, well …"

"You think Andie did it?"

God, was she letting a territorial tendency toward Chad get the better of her? "I don't know." Jen blew the steam away from the top of her mug.

"What did she say? Maybe you need to tell the police."

"No. It's probably nothing. I'm just … she mentioned something about Chad not dating employees because someone named Tasha nearly ruined him." She shrugged. "I don't know. I didn't get the chance to talk to Chad." Not true. She had plenty of chances, but her mouth had been otherwise occupied.

Zoe frowned. "I remember Tasha. She stole a lot of money from the diner, and Chad took a lot of heat from the family for dating an employee and giving her too much freedom."

Her heart hurt, her head throbbed, and something kept telling her this diner thing was connected to her. Maybe the confrontation in the bathroom and Jen leaving with Chad pushed Andie over the edge.

The bell at the door chimed.

"Morning, Ash," Zoe called out.

"I'm glad you didn't say 'good.' What a fiasco, huh?"

Ashley stood beside Jen, who was still looking for answers in the bottom of a cup of coffee.

"I take it you were over there," Zoe said.

Ashley nodded.

Zoe sighed. "I'm worried it's my dad."

"That's not what I heard. Uncle Richard said it was Chad."

"Chad?" Jen lifted her head and widened her eyes. The only thing keeping her in her seat was the counter.

"Chad said he was rushing to get out of the diner yesterday and left linens in the dryer. I guess with all the grease and oil they can smolder for hours if not taken out, and then they can spontaneously combust."

She couldn't bear to delete the text messages that proved how anxious he'd been to get out of the diner and home ... to her. It *was* her fault. Inadvertently, maybe. But still.

"If I didn't know any better, I'd think he was cursed," Ashley said, accepting a cup of coffee from Zoe.

No, Jen was the cursed one, and it was time she broke the spell that was holding her here and keeping Chad at risk.

Chapter Fourteen

Chad didn't see why Jen had to leave. There was nothing more he could do about the diner until the fire investigation was complete, which meant he had the rest of the day to crawl back into bed and hopefully wake up outside this nightmare.

He wanted to wake up with her.

"It's too long of a drive when you're tired," he said, holding onto her bag so she couldn't go.

"I'll be fine. I'll call when I'm home."

How long would it be until Emerald Springs was her home? Last night, holding her in his arms, he felt powerful enough to convince her to stay—from that moment on. Now, the truth was out about his lack of judgment with Tasha and his questionable start with Andie, and Jen was pulling away. It wasn't a coincidence.

Dropping the suitcase, he held her by the upper arms. "None of this has anything to do with you."

Her watery gaze searched somewhere over his head. "It feels like it does."

Because those run-ins with Andie led Jen to label herself the latest shiny thing to distract him from his diner duties.

"Jen ... " He touched his forehead to her forehead.

"I just need some space and perspective."

Why did that worry him? Maybe getting out of Emerald Springs while he was sorting through this was the best thing she could do.

"A lot has happened this weekend," she said.

He smiled because he couldn't argue. "A lot of good things."

He wasn't going to lose sight of that, especially if she was. Someone had to see what this could be if they held on through the rough parts.

She smiled, but it didn't sparkle in her eyes. "I need to go."

He didn't agree, but he dropped his hands from her arms and straightened.

While she flattened a garment bag on the back seat, he tucked an envelope with her final consulting paycheck in the front pocket of her suitcase and then lifted the bag into the trunk.

"Pull over if you get tired, and call me with where you stopped." He gathered her into his arms before she could get into the car.

"I'm not going to stop," she said against his chest, and though she was tense when he pulled her close, the longer she stayed there, the softer she felt.

He buried his lips and nose in her hair. She smelled like tea and hops. Maybe he was imagining it, but the scents were so clear. She was made for him.

"I ... " *love you.*

She jerked away at the sound of his voice, like she could read his mind and didn't want to hear what he was going to say.

" ... have to go," she finished. "You're supposed to be meeting with your dad."

He was, but this was important, too.

Unfortunately, the moment passed. Looking at her troubled face, it was clear if he said the words now, she would run for good.

She'd told him she didn't like surprises. Well, he was seeing that firsthand.

Jen slipped into the driver's seat, clutching the wheel with both hands. "Thank you for everything."

She didn't look at him.

Fear clogged his arteries, but he battled the pinch in his heart and leaned into the car, kissing her on the cheek. "I'll see you soon." It was a promise.

She nodded.

Closing the door on her was something he couldn't do, so he stepped back and let her do the job.

He was still standing in the same place long after she'd driven away.

When his phone rang, he startled, snatching it from his back pocket, hoping beyond reason it was her. When he saw it was Dad, he answered with chin up and shoulders back. He had a microbrewery to build. The faster he was brewing beer, the faster Jen would return—for good.

Once he was sitting at the long table in the farm office, flanked by Adam and Daniel, staring at a solemn-faced Dad, Chad felt the gravity of the situation.

"We're not going to be able to touch the property until the investigation is finished, a cause is determined, and everything is squared away with insurance," Dad said.

"Meaning the microbrewery is delayed," Adam added.

Chad didn't need the lead in. He understood what he was up against now. "Delayed until when?"

Dad shrugged. "Right now, I'd say indefinitely."

He fought the disappointment, threatening to yank him from his seat and send him off in search of something more pleasant. A hike, a beer, a drive to Seattle—to Jen. After all, without the microbrewery, what did he have to look forward to here?

"Construction is just delayed until insurance is settled, correct?" Daniel asked.

Chad didn't even care about the answer. *Tomato. Tomahto.* Indefinitely sounded like a death sentence to him. And why shouldn't it be? The idea his family would plunk millions of dollars into his lap after he nearly burned down the diner was laughable. In the last two months, he'd been captain of a ship that had seen two brawls and a fire.

The sound that came from Chad's mouth was anything but a laugh. God, he could finally, clearly see the mess his family had been seeing.

Daniel gripped the back of Chad's neck like Dad would do. "We'll get through this."

He didn't know how. And yet, he'd heard those words before. Over and over again when Mom died. As much as this delay sucked, Daniel was right. They'd get through it. If they made it through losing Mom, this would be a piece of Zoe Miller's chocolate cake.

But that didn't mean what waited on the other side wasn't going to suck. Jen needed a job, a job he didn't have to offer now, a job he might never have to offer if "indefinitely" remained true. How could he expect her to walk away from brewing, something she loved and lived for, just for a shot at life in Emerald Springs with him?

"What do we do about Andie?" Adam asked.

It just kept getting worse.

Chad roughed his face in his hands. He still believed he was to blame for the fire, but the inspector was investigating all angles, including Andie. No matter what he thought about her behavior a day ago, when faced with carrying out the dirty work, he wasn't sure he could. If he fired her, he'd be responsible for two women without a livelihood. And Andie was a single mother.

"She needs that job," Chad said, dropping his hands, coming up for air.

"We can't keep her on if she had anything to do with this." Dad looked so sure of his judgment call. There were consequences to actions. He'd told Chad that time and time again.

Chad's stomach pitched because it was a double standard—all the second chances his family was willing to give him. "But you'll keep me on if I had something to do with it?"

"Son, if it was you, it was an accident."

"No." That wasn't a fair assessment. If it was him, it was neglect. Maybe it wasn't the same thing as arson, but it was bad nonetheless.

"I'm telling you right now, I expect the same punishment you'd want me to hand down to an employee."

Silence echoed around him. It was tantamount to their disagreement, but he knew they knew: if they didn't fire him, he'd quit.

Either way, he'd finally get what he deserved.

• • •

Upon returning home, Jen slept for eight hours straight. She woke up to the moon outside her bedroom window and a vicious hunger in her gut.

Not knowing if Mara and Mick were behind the closed door across the hall, she tiptoed to the kitchen to feast on mint chocolate chip ice cream. With her legs tucked beneath her and her mouth frozen from the feast, she stared into the darkness of the living room, listening only to her breathing.

She didn't want to be here, but she didn't want to be in Emerald Springs, not under the current circumstances.

What *did* she want?

She wanted to run away, which wasn't surprising … but she wanted Chad by her side. That was a first—wanting someone else to go with her. Maybe he'd be game. Maybe after all this, he'd hop a flight with her to Colorado and see what came next.

It was a happy sentiment—one amid a sea of miserable ones.

"Hey, I thought I heard someone out here."

Jen glanced at Mara's shadow coming closer to the couch. "Who else would it be?"

"Mick. He's supposed to come here after closing the bar."

Apparently their weekend had gone well. That was good. Really. Jen refused to add jealousy to her weekend.

Mara sat. "The early hour and the ice cream don't look good. What happened?"

"A lot." Jen considered getting up and going back to bed, but Mara would follow.

"Did you sleep with him?"

"I did."

Mara snagged the spoon from the container and helped herself. "Since you're not gushing, I'm going to assume that didn't go well."

"I don't gush, and it was great." Only the word *great* prompted any real reaction from Jen, sticking in her throat, filling her head with memories. The way he smelled, the way he tasted, the way he touched her in ethereal places she didn't even know she had.

She'd never loved and accepted herself—body and soul—like she had when she was with Chad. Maybe that made her pathetic.

Jen snatched the spoon from Mara and dug into the ice cream again.

"So if the sex was great, then why aren't you? What else happened?"

The cold cream numbed her brain, letting the rest spill out easily. "There was a fire at the diner."

"Holy shit! Was anyone hurt?"

"Not physically." It was too early to assess the complete emotional toll, but if her inner turmoil was any indication, there would be plenty of hurt to go around.

"How'd it happen?"

"They don't know for sure. Chad thinks he did it by accident when he left towels in the dryer." She tapped the heel of the spoon against her bottom teeth. "But I think his assistant manager did it because she was jealous of him being with me."

"Damn." Mara stood. "I need my own spoon."

They polished off the carton while Jen relayed the rest of the weekend's details. Her head was as stuffed as her stomach.

"What now?" Mara asked.

"I don't know." Jen set the empty carton on the coffee table and pulled a pillow to her chest.

"But Chad wants to make this thing between you work?"

"He does, but that doesn't mean it should." How many times had Jen said those exact words when it came to Mick and Mara?

Mara rested her head on Jen's shoulder. "It's good to work through the rough stuff, because when you do, you appreciate the good stuff even more."

Jen wouldn't know. She'd never stuck around long enough to see what came after the rough stuff. The rough stuff was always enough to push her away. And right now, she was done with this. If the topic didn't change, she was going to walk away from Mara, too.

"How was your weekend?" Jen asked.

Mara sighed.

It was the non-verbal equivalent to *wonderful*. Jen cringed as she rode a wave of unwanted jealousy.

"We came to a compromise," Mara said. "If he's going to continue working hard to make the bar a success, he isn't going to continue living above it. There's no separation when he's in the same building."

"Where's he going to live?" Jen knew the answer before Mara opened her mouth.

"Well, it makes sense for him to move in here if you're moving to Emerald Springs." She grabbed Jen's hand. "But if that's not going to happen, we'll figure something else out."

And Jen would be alone—again. Which was probably for the best. If nobody got messed up with her, then nobody got messed up.

"What did my mother have to say?" Might as well finish up with the most unpalatable conversation of all.

"She liked my hair and noticed I'd lost some weight."

"She always was superficial."

Mara chuckled. "She also said she misses you and hopes you're happy."

Jen winced so hard her neck hurt.

A key jiggled in the lock and Mara straightened. "I can tell him to go home."

"Don't be ridiculous."

Mara smacked a hand to Jen's thigh and went to meet Mick.

Jen curled into a ball on the couch, covered in darkness, listening to their whispers and happy kisses on the way to Mara's bedroom.

It was soul shattering because she wanted that, too, but she was afraid after everything, it was impossible.

When the sun rose, she woke, stretching arms overhead, feeling better than she had last night.

Better was a relative word.

She saw her suitcase and garment bag where she'd left them beside the entertainment center. Meaning to drag them to her room and unpack, she crossed the room. It was then she saw a white envelope sticking out of the front pocket of the suitcase. She didn't recall putting anything there.

Of course, *she* hadn't. The white, business envelope with a clear address window revealed her name and address. It was an Emerald Springs Farm paycheck. She'd received one before. She'd been due another, but honestly, after everything, she expected Chad to mail it.

Her finger split the seal, and she freed the check, coming face to face with a handwritten note across the ledger portion of the paycheck.

We make a great team. Thank you for everything. Love, Chad

It wasn't anything he hadn't said to her before, except … *love*, which may or may not have meant anything. And yet, she stood there, staring at his handwriting, choking on tears she refused to shed.

Now she had a physical reminder of the way he felt. It was the way she felt, too.

They did make a great team. She was thankful for everything. And whether or not Chad meant the salutation, she loved him. Even without the vice grip on her heart, it was true. Otherwise, she would've walked away for good a long time ago.

She'd never had a problem cutting ties before.

So what came next? Feeling love for someone and revealing love to someone were very different things under the best circumstances. As if the first thought didn't already scare her enough, the idea of acting on the second thought left her in tatters.

She tossed the paycheck on the desk as she passed.

It was too much right now. She was going to unpack, take a shower, and follow up on the interview invitation in Colorado.

If the job in Emerald Springs evaporated, she needed to be prepared.

Chapter Fifteen

Chad needed to see Jen even more than he needed to get out of the pressure cooker in Emerald Springs. Thank God she agreed to have dinner with him. Honestly, he wasn't sure she would. After the way she left at the beginning of the week, a big part of him expected her to turn him down in the spirit of more space and perspective. Heck, after the meeting with Dad, he had to battle tooth and nail with himself to rationalize this weekend trip.

Talk about a change in perspective.

The two-hour drive to Seattle filled him with hope that there was still a chance for them, but as he sat across from her in an Italian restaurant, he questioned the optimism.

She wasn't herself, and he wasn't himself, either.

"The ravioli is good here." She kept her face half-shielded by the lunch menu.

Thirty minutes into their meeting, and they still hadn't talked about anything substantial.

Nodding, he stared so hard at his menu the letters blurred. They weren't going to get past this if they couldn't even talk about it.

He slouched in the booth, because he was as much to blame for the avoidance as she was. He didn't want to get into the serious stuff only to be interrupted by the waitress.

Biting his tongue, Chad weathered the small talk.

Once their orders were taken and their glasses were filled, Chad reached across the table and took Jen's hand. "I miss you."

She smiled, but it looked uncomfortable. "I miss you, too."

"I dream about driving up here at least once a day, and I would if I thought it was what you wanted me to do." His thumb rode her knuckles.

"I want you to take care of the diner"—her brow wrinkled—"so you can move on to the microbrewery."

He exhaled. "There's not much I can do. I'm at the mercy of inspectors, the insurance company, and, of course, my dad."

She didn't look surprised. In fact, the wrinkles disappeared from her brow the moment he spoke his concerns. Apparently, they'd been her concerns, too.

"So everything's up in the air?"

No, not everything. He still loved her, wanted her, saw his future with her despite an inability to figure out how that could work if the microbrewery fell through.

He squeezed her hand. "The microbrewery is up in the air, yes."

She looked away into the busy dining room and then she shrugged. "So we wait."

"We do."

Her wrinkles returned. She faced him again, but she wasn't exactly looking at him. "I'm going to keep the interview in Colorado."

He shouldn't have been surprised. She needed a job. Under these precarious circumstances what had he expected her to do? But it felt like she was losing faith in him—in them. It sucked, because after a lifetime of not giving a damn, he was losing faith in himself, too. And he couldn't let that happen—not when he finally realized how good life could be when he buckled down and took it seriously.

"You don't need to do that. It's going to work out. I'm going to make sure it works out."

She pulled her hand from his. "But just in case, I need to have a backup plan."

It was only an interview. Hiring people took time. By then, he should have a better idea of what was happening with *his* microbrewery, and he'd have a job offer that would make the other one pale in comparison. Until then, he was done with the misery.

"Let's do something fun," he said when he settled the check.

She raised a brow, looking intrigued and interested for the first time all day. "Like what?" And then her lips curved. "My apartment is already occupied, you know."

He bounced out of his seat at the flirtation in her voice, and offered a hand. "Get your mind out of the gutter, Chavez. There are other things we can do for fun."

She took his hand, but rolled her eyes. "Like what?"

"You'll see."

An hour later he was staring at Jen's ass bound in a zip line harness.

She glanced over her shoulder at him. "See you at the bottom, baby."

Right then and there, with that smile lingering in his brain, he had enough motivation to win any battle they faced.

On a signal, he pushed off the platform, grinning like a maniac. This was exactly what they needed, a little fresh air, free flying, and time alone. Wind rushed him, slipping beneath his helmet and the sleeves of his shirt. He heard Jen squeal ahead of him as he gripped the T-bar, lifted his face to the sky, and let out a whoop of his own.

From up here at a steady speed, the landscape blended together—leaves as far as the eye could see. The gory details of life seemed manageable, laughable really, with something this exhilarating to put them in perspective.

All too soon he was tucking his legs to his chest and readying to meet the dirt path.

Jen was waiting nearby. Her harness and helmet had been removed, but the smile stayed firm on her face.

He waited until the line crew removed his gear before he trotted to her.

"How about that?" he asked with eyebrows bobbing. "Fun comes in many forms."

She laughed. "This was great. I'll give you that."

"I sense a but here."

She shook her head and walked.

He walked alongside her, his heart still pounding with adrenaline.

"No but." The heaviness from earlier had left her voice. "It was fun." She looked up at him, eyes shining.

He took her hand, swinging their arms back and forth as they walked under the cover of trees.

He didn't want to leave. He didn't want this to end. But she had a roommate, and he had an inoperable diner that needed to be turned into a microbrewery, where Jen could work.

If he wanted both things, he needed to handle them responsibly.

"I don't want to go, but I should get back," he said, squeezing her hand.

She stopped their arms from swinging. "I know."

"Could I convince you to come with me?"

Her eyes softened to wide and sultry. "Probably without much effort … if I didn't have this trip to Colorado planned."

He grimaced. Talk about a mood crusher. But then she wrapped herself around his arm and leaned her head against him, perking him up again.

"It's a contingency plan," she said. "I still want to brew with you."

Halting his steps, Chad lifted her chin so he could see her face. "So I'm your first choice?"

"Definitely."

He backed her off the path and into the trees amid laughter. Using the widest trunk, he shielded them from the path, kissing the smile right off her face. He pressed his full length against her and pinned her arms overhead while he plundered her mouth.

By the time he was done with her, he was going to be the only choice.

•••

Jen returned to her apartment a little breathless, a little dazed. There must have been a dozen heated kisses between the zip line park and her place, not to mention two very satisfying orgasms in an out-of-the-way part of the parking lot.

She was simultaneously thankful and disappointed to find Mick and Mara gone. Had she known, she would've invited Chad in for "one more for the road." She smiled, tossed her purse on the sofa, and went off in search of some cold water.

Standing by the sink, guzzling from a glass, she prayed this Emerald Springs microbrewery thing worked out. Otherwise, she might do something stupid like consider giving up the career she loved to be with a man.

When a knock sounded at the door, her pulse jumped. Chad. The way he'd been insatiable in the woods and in the car, she could see him turning around and pushing his way in here.

She grinned as she rushed to the door.

Her smile twisted when she came face to face with her mother.

"Baby girl!" A blast of nauseating perfume hit Jen before Mom's arms did. They wound around her neck so tightly, Jen was sure she'd faint from lack of air.

When she was finally free, she was standing in the middle of her living room, too far away from the door to easily manipulate the woman back out.

"You're still in Seattle." It was a statement born of shock. What if Chad had stayed?

Mom smiled as though she didn't have a care in the world. Dressed in a sparkly pantsuit she most certainly couldn't afford and a pair of ridiculously-high espadrilles, her life was apparently perfect as she stood in Jen's apartment.

She extended her arms to her sides and took a deep breath. "The air out here is good for my complexion."

Jen breathed, too, because if she didn't, the anxiety building inside of her was going to explode like a nuclear bomb.

Talk to her. Humor her. She'll be gone soon.

Surprise visits like this one happened. They never lasted longer than it took for Gloria to be assuaged of guilt over neglecting Jen.

"Can I get you something to drink?" she asked, going through the motions.

"That would be lovely. Chardonnay?"

Chardonnay … for a woman who spent decades strung out on cheap beer … for a woman whose daughter was a brewmaster? Jen shook her head. "I have beer, and I have vodka. The vodka I can mix with orange juice."

"Ooh, the vodka sounds perfect."

When she returned from the kitchen, Mom sat on the sofa, an eager look on her made-up face. "Where were you? Mara said you were out of town. For work?"

"Yep." She handed her a tumbler.

"I didn't realize there was travel in your line of work."

"I'm doing some consulting."

"Does it pay well?"

It always came down to money.

"Enough to cover the bills," Jen said, drinking deeply from her bottle of beer.

Mom drank too, eyeing up the apartment. There was no hint of disapproval on her face, but this was not the kind of life Gloria would choose.

"So, where are you staying?" Jen asked, even though a large portion of her didn't want to know.

"Four Seasons. A friend of mine has connections there."

She nodded while she drank some more. The friend probably rented Mom a luxury car, too.

She could only imagine how that debt would be settled.

"How long are you here?" Considering Mom was here longer than Jen already expected, anxiety wrapped around each word.

Gloria widened her eyes and smacked her lips. "Surprise! It's open-ended. Isn't that wonderful?"

She coughed, sending beer surging back into her throat, burning her nose. "It'll be like Miami, baby," Mom cooed. "You and me against the world."

Jen continued to cough, even though the urge had passed. "I need water," she finally managed.

And then she was gone, hyperventilating in the kitchen, wishing she wasn't three stories off the ground so she could jump out the window and never return.

"Ooh, baby girl! What's this? 'We make a great team. Thanks for everything. Love, Chad.'"

Shit! She'd left the check and note on the desk in plain sight. Mom was going to jump all over this. She rushed into the living room.

"It's nothing."

Gloria's eyes widened and her lips curved. "Is he your boyfriend?"

"My boss," Jen spouted out of a sense of protection, snatching the check from her mother's hand.

"Even better." Gloria clapped, her long red fingernails looking more and more like claws.

"It's not like that." But it was. And Jen hoped to God the heat in her throat didn't reach her complexion and give her away.

"What do you mean it's not like that? Of course it's like that. Your boss leaves cutesie notes on your paycheck. What else would it be?"

"None of your business."

Gloria laughed. "Are you *friends*?" She dragged out the word, making it sound dirty.

"It's none of your business," she said again, more emphatically this time.

"Oh, come on. I'm your mother. I'm proud of you. I'm happy to see you finally doing something about your depressing living conditions. It's about time you thought about your future."

Words failed her. It figured the most pride she'd ever garner from this woman would be for something seedy. And why not? Sleeping with the boss was right up Gloria Chavez's alley.

"Wait a minute." Mom snapped her fingers and her jaw dropped. "Emerald Springs Farm, like Emerald Tea? You're brewing tea?"

"No, I'm not."

"What are you … hey! I read an article about the Whitmans in a magazine. The father is a widower, and he has three unmarried sons." She squealed. "This is good, baby. Real good."

There was a ruckus at the door, and Mara and Mick pushed inside. They froze at the scene.

"Hey," Mara rushed to Jen's side, friendliness in her voice but defensiveness on her face.

Gloria was all over Mick in five … four … three … two … one.

He might not be rich—yet—but he was too handsome for Gloria to ignore.

"What the fuck?" Mara whispered while Mick kept Mom busy.

Jen squeezed her eyes shut. She was living her worst nightmare.

Chapter Sixteen

This was not the way Jen wanted to return to Emerald Springs. She tossed and turned last night, dreaming about Chad—how she would tell him, how she would protect him.

Mom had returned. Worse, she was staying in Seattle. Two hours away wasn't enough of a buffer from Emerald Springs for Gloria not to wreak havoc, especially if Jen was working at the Whitmans' microbrewery, giving her easy access to the Whitman family.

Mara kept saying it wasn't that bad. After all, Chad already knew Gloria was no June Cleaver. Mick kept cracking cougar jokes after his second run-in with the first-class flirt. But deep inside, Jen knew the truth.

This was a disaster waiting to happen.

She'd been kidding herself believing anything permanent could happen between her and Chad. Emerald Springs wasn't some impenetrable hamlet where she could hide in peace and grow old in harmony. Gloria would find her. She'd show up, flash a smile and some boob, destroy numerous relationships, and then walk out of town with a gazillion bucks she didn't earn, leaving Jen to pick up the pieces.

She would vow never to brew another beer before she would lead her mother to Emerald Springs.

More than liking the Whitmans, she respected them. They were the kind of family she'd always wished she'd had—and that was why she let herself get carried away.

It was time to get back on track. This didn't start out as a search for some ridiculous fairy tale. This had been about paying the bills. She'd received her last paycheck, so it was time to move on.

Jen reached the farm office with her mission clear: she would personally and respectfully decline Mr. Whitman's generous offer to be brewmaster, rather than blow out of town without another word, reflecting poorly on Chad. Thanks to Tasha and Andie, he'd had enough of that from women in his past. She didn't want to add to that list.

Walking the corridor to Mr. Whitman's office, Jen fought her panic. Once she did this, there would be no turning back. Mr. Whitman would hear the news first, then Chad. They might get angry. Certainly Chad would be hurt. But, that would be better than being lied to and stolen from. Which was exactly what would happen if Mom got her chance.

And she wouldn't. With Jen gone, Gloria would move on—maybe follow Jen to Colorado. Oh, the memories that were associated with that. But the Whitmans would be safe. Even if she made some sort of bold move to access the Whitmans in Jen's absence, Chad knew the truth, and he'd protect his family. He could use any means necessary if Jen and her feelings weren't around to consider.

Chad was just the kind of guy who would refuse to press changes on someone who stole from him. Jen clenched her hands. *No way.* She was doing the right things, being here, going there.

"Jen, it's lovely to see you." The hearty voice took her by surprise. She didn't know why. It wasn't like Mr. Whitman to be any other way. Maybe she expected him to discover her reason for coming with one look at her face.

"Mr. Whitman." She shook his hand. "Thank you for meeting with me on such short notice."

He waved her off. "Anytime."

His smile made her hesitate. It was the kind of smile she used to dream about when she dreamed about having a father. But one visit from Gloria would wipe that eager smile off his face.

"What can I do for you?" he asked.

"Well, sir." She clenched her teeth for a second, hoping to calm the quiver in her voice. "I wanted to personally thank you again for the brewmaster job offer. It's very generous of you."

"Nonsense. You're qualified."

She was. God, how she wished that was the only concern.

"I can't accept the position," she said in a voice that wasn't nearly as strong and determined as she'd hoped it would be.

"I see." He motioned for her to sit. "Is there anything I can do to change your mind?"

She sat, summoning courage enough to walk away from good people like this. "No. It's … because of … my family."

"I hope everything is okay."

It wasn't, but she didn't need to tell him that.

"Colorado is a better fit for my family." *Because it's farther away from your family.*

He studied her as he nodded. "I can't say I'm not disappointed. It seems like such a shame you won't be able to reap the benefits of your hard work." He tapped a stack of papers beside him. "This is one of the most inspired and thorough business plans I've ever seen."

She smiled at that. Who knew she had entrepreneurial blood in her body?

"Thank you," she managed. "But Chad deserves most of the praise. I just talked about beer as much as I could."

Mr. Whitman gave his head a jovial shake and then leaned back in his chair, studying her. "What does my son have to say about this?"

Jen swallowed the thick emotion gathering in her throat at the sound of his name. She didn't want to think about him, let alone think about what he would say about this. He wasn't going to be happy.

"I haven't talked to him, yet." She squirmed, shoving her hands between clenched thighs. "I wanted to see you first. I appreciate the faith you've had in me and the way you've welcomed me … " Even after she hit his car and hit on his son. "Coming here and relaying my decision in person seemed like the right thing to do."

She reached into her purse, pulled out a business envelope, and placed it on his desk.

"What's this?"

"My final paycheck. It should cover the damage to your truck."

He touched the very edge of the paper, and for a second she expected him to push it back, but then he patted it and smiled at her. "That's very honorable, young lady. Thank you." He stood and reached an outstretched hand across the desk. "I wish you all the luck in the world."

She was going to need it.

The worst part was yet to come.

Back in her car, she drove in the opposite direction of Chad's house for several yards. The highway was calling her name. But she pulled into a vacant lot. He deserved more than her disappearance. Besides, if she disappeared, he would surely call, and the lingering connection would make things worse. Clean breaks were easier.

She'd learned about clean breaks from her dad. After he left, he never once tried to contact her. It sucked, but then it didn't—it was almost like he'd never been there in the first place. Too bad she couldn't say the same for her mom, who jumped in and out of Jen's life, leaving the longest, heaviest chain wrapped around her neck—all the woman had to do was yank it hard enough to upend Jen's world.

With one hand around her throat and the other guiding the steering wheel, Jen turned the car toward Chad's.

Clean break. She hoped she had the guts to go through with it.

• • •

"What are you doing here?" Chad hopped off the porch and jogged to Jen, who was standing in his driveway. He didn't wait for her to answer. He gathered her in his arms and squeezed. "I don't care what you say, surprises are awesome."

But then it hit him. She wasn't hugging back. In fact, she was stiff, holding her face away from his neck.

He set her on the ground amid a rush of dread and closed his eyes. *Please, don't let this be as bad as it feels.*

When he looked at her, he saw tears.

"What?" The word stuck in his throat.

"Can we go inside?"

She was leaving … for good. He could feel it in his gut.

Looking around at nothing but fields and trees as far as his eyes could see, he succumbed to anger. "No."

If she was going to rip his heart out, he'd rather it not be in his house. He had enough trouble sleeping already without adding ugly memories of this to the mix.

"Fine." She exhaled out her open mouth. "I just talked to your dad."

Chad stepped back, confused, shoving his hands in his pockets. He expected some good-bye speech, some job announcement that didn't involve Emerald Springs. He didn't expect the rundown of a conversation she had with his dad.

"This is … hard, so please don't interrupt me."

He couldn't if he wanted to. His mouth was so dry he couldn't swallow, let alone speak.

"I'm going to take the job in Colorado … if they want me."

He was right. Lucky him. The sarcastic thought burned a hole in his heart.

"Why?" he asked. Whether she had bills to pay or not, throwing away a chance at building this dream together seemed like such a waste. "If it's about money, I can help you out with that."

"No." She pounced on his words like they were an insult. "I will not take your money."

"I'll put you on payroll like everyone else at the diner who is laid off because of the fire. What's the big deal?"

She shook her head. "No. I was hired as a consultant. I was paid as a consultant. My job is done."

"So this was just a job?" The question sounded like a sneer.

She lifted her chin. "Yes."

"Liar."

She grinned. The joyless expression made his skin crawl. "I told you I was a liar, didn't I?" She looked crazed, pulling at the roots of her hair. "I told you if I got the chance I'd lie and cheat and steal. Well, there's your proof." Her last word echoed on the wind.

He closed his eyes and dropped his chin to his chest. This was unreal. The ugliest surge of anger rose to strangle him.

"I'm sorry. I never wanted to hurt you." She sniffled every word.

He took in her disheveled appearance again and told himself to keep cool … give her the benefit of the doubt … something wasn't adding up here. For some reason, she thought taking another job and pushing him away was what she needed to do.

But no matter how many times he repeated those words and no matter how many breaths he took, he couldn't calm the fury.

"That's the biggest bunch of bullshit I've ever heard," he hissed.

"Chad, don't."

"Don't what?" He was yelling now; so much for keeping cool. "Don't fight for this—for us? I'm sorry, but I thought we were worth it."

It was her turn to hang her head. He wished he could be heroic enough to lift her chin and kiss her mouth, but his rage at the fact she didn't believe in them enough to fight froze him in place.

There was absolutely no good reason for her to bow out of this microbrewery job before the fire inspector came to a conclusion. What if construction started next week?

"There's more to your story, isn't there?" He breathed through his open mouth, struggling to calm the turmoil.

She shrugged and then shook her head, refusing to make eye contact. "Colorado is a better fit."

"Again, bullshit. I know there's more." Her panic reminded him of the night of the engagement party … and suddenly it all made sense. "This has something to do with your mother, doesn't it?"

"Of course it does." She threw the words at him.

"Then tell me what's going on. Tell me everything. I want you to look me in the eye and tell me why you're really running away."

She growled, but she looked at him. "I'm protecting you."

He growled back. "You're killing me."

She paced his dirt driveway, huffing with every step until finally she exploded. "You have no idea what you're talking about. Not only is my mother *in* Washington, she says she's *staying* in Washington. What do you think of that?"

Surprise. It was a bad joke. After the way Jen reacted to text messages about her mother, he could imagine what seeing the woman could do. Heck, he didn't have to imagine it—he was witnessing the fallout right here.

None of it was pretty, but it had to be resolvable. Taking advantage of a break in his anger, he stepped toward her.

She stepped away from him.

Her rejection toppled his reprieve.

"If I stay and give her easy access to you, she will ruin you," Jen said.

"She won't get the chance. You're doing it for her." He was shaking now, the veins in his arms bulging blue beneath his skin. "Does it even matter that I love you?"

She pushed her arms into her gut and bent a bit, like his words hurt. He hoped they did because he wasn't feeling warm and fuzzy, either.

Misery loved company, baby.

"I'm sorry," she said, and then she scrambled to her car.

"Coward," he called after her, but he didn't move a muscle to stop her.

He had some pride left.

Jen looked at him over the grimy metal roof. Her tears glistened in the sun. The way she stared told him she wanted to say more, and in his heart he felt the words.

She loved him, too, and this stupid attempt at martyrdom was the result.

Before he could figure out how to stop her, she was gone, peeling down the dirt road, swirls of dust in her wake.

Chad made it as far as the porch before he collapsed on the top step.

Dropping his face to his hands, he roared. He had to go after her.

But he didn't move.

Going after her wasn't going to change the crippling issues she had with her mother, and as long as those were there, Jen's first response was always going to be *run*. She'd proved time and time again he wasn't enough to stop her.

Reality seeped in, leaving him more heartbroken than angry.

Lying back on the porch, he stared at the wooden ceiling. His eyes burned. His heart ached. And his head felt ready to explode.

She thought she was sacrificing herself for him. He had news for her … she just sacrificed everything for nothing.

Chapter Seventeen

It had been years since Jen had been in Colorado. After graduation, she'd latched onto an internship in Wisconsin with help from Professor Krem. Then, a job offer came from Washington. She'd wanted to brew so badly, she took the job even though she'd wanted to come back here. Denver had been her escape from Miami. It was where she'd found freedom and a future—until her mother came to town.

But that was a long time ago. Professor Krem wasn't even in Denver anymore. She could start over here.

Staring out the rental car window at the mountains speckled with snow, she forced herself to smile. Maybe the physical show of happiness would translate into something hopeful on the inside.

It failed to do anything more than make her lips tingle.

It's going to take time.

Less than twenty-four hours ago she said goodbye to her dream job and the man who loved her. An angry vein had been bulging in his forehead when he shouted the words, so the moment was more shocking than it was romantic … at least that's what she told herself.

While those three little words stopped her in her tracks, they weren't enough to derail her. Chad didn't need her hanging around causing him more trouble.

And he didn't need to know she loved him, too.

Love wouldn't change the fact Gloria was prowling around Washington State without a job. *Ha!* That made two Chavez women desperate for a paycheck.

Jen gave up on the smile and turned into Mountain Pass Brewery. Standing alone between a strip mall and a quick-change oil place, it was uninspired—nothing like the microbrewery she and Chad had planned to build.

The comparison left a bad taste in her mouth.

It's unfair to judge.

But she judged anyway. She wrinkled her nose as she pulled open the door to find a pretty blonde with a pair of green eyes smiling at her from behind a sleek, granite counter.

"Welcome to Mountain Pass Brewery." The hostess was wearing a cleavage-popping, black mini-dress … with pearls.

Pearls did not belong in a microbrewery. And that wasn't even taking into consideration the seductive dress.

"Hi. I'm Jen Chavez, and I'm here to meet with Gretchen Collier."

"One moment please." The woman lifted a phone to her ear.

While she waited, Jen scanned the rest of the building. She recognized one spot from the single, website photo—the massive granite bar—but nothing else seemed familiar. In fact, without the spread of food and mugs of beer featured in the picture, this place looked a little too upscale for a microbrewery. If the name Mountain Pass Brewery wasn't frosted on the door glass, she'd have sworn she was in the wrong place. There wasn't anything mountain-y or brewery about it.

"Ms. Chavez, JoJo will take you to Gretchen."

Jen turned.

JoJo was a mirror image of the blonde with no name. Another skintight black dress, cleavage, and pearls. It was the Hooters of microbreweries.

How did she not pick that up from the website?

Jen's eyebrows rose, but she smiled to hide the sarcasm in her expression.

As they walked, she studied the trendy surroundings, trying to locate anything that gave away the fact this was a microbrewery. Other than a few beers on patrons' tables, there was nothing.

"So you're interviewing for the brewmaster position? How cool."

Jen nodded. *You'd think so, huh?* But she was a little off her game. She was still reeling from the events in Emerald Springs and finding little comfort here.

JoJo greeted a passing server who was outfitted in the same ridiculous, distracting outfit. Probably a marketing trick to mask the sucky beer. "Uniform" or not, it made Jen squirm in her sweater dress, tights, and riding boots.

"Right through here." JoJo parted a beaded curtain and held one side so she could pass through.

Classical music filled the hall. *Classical music.* Jen shook her head, but she smiled in case it was some sort of hidden camera test.

"Gretchen," JoJo said as she knocked on a sleek, black door.

The door swung open and—surprise—another overly dressed, pretty woman smiled at Jen. "Come in. Come in."

They exchanged the customary greetings. *How was your trip? I'm glad you could make it. I'm glad to be here.*

That last one was becoming a bigger lie with each passing second.

What Jen really wanted to say was *what the hell was the owner thinking?* But she zipped her lips and sat instead, hoping this wasn't a wasted trip.

They talked about beer, Jen's Lovely Lady Honey Ale mostly, and about her connections to Boulder. They talked about brewing in a male-dominated field. They talked about the explosion of craft brews, the proliferation of microbreweries, and the dichotomy of success in the industry.

Jen was well-versed in the business side of things, thanks to the contract work she'd done for Chad. Her interviewing nerves receded enough to allow a little pinch in her heart. She'd put everything she had into the plans for Emerald Springs' microbrewery. It seemed cruel she wouldn't be brewing there.

"This is wonderful," Gretchen gushed. "So you'll totally see what we're trying to do here."

"What *are* you trying to do here?" she asked, careful to smile away any harshness in her voice.

"Well, we're turning the tables so to speak. Under the guidance of new management, we're taking a targeted male population and giving them what they want—tits, ass, and beer—" she grinned, "so we can make what we want in return." She rubbed the tips of her fingers together in the universal sign for money. "It's about embracing femininity in a setting suitable for professional, male clientele with deep pockets."

Jen blinked. Wasn't that the theory behind "gentlemen's clubs"?

This wasn't a microbrewery. This was a restaurant where pretty, scantily clad women served businessmen overpriced craft beer. And they didn't even own up to it in public. Nothing on the website alluded to this marketing twist. Then again, maybe the website hadn't caught up with the new management's idea.

"Do you have questions," Gretchen asked.

Too many to count. "I do," she said. "Exactly how many beers do you brew … and where? I didn't see any brewing equipment."

Gretchen smiled that perfect smile. "We brew offsite to keep the smell and clutter down. But don't worry, I've been wanting to institute something a little different that will have the brewmaster in-house on Monday, Friday, and Saturday nights. I call it: *date with the brewmaster.*"

Her jaw dropped, and Gretchen chuckled.

"It's not like that. You won't actually be dating them—unless you work something out on the side." She winked. "And I don't want to know about that if you do. As far as I'm concerned, you'll just go from table to table and flirt, talk about the beer, and get them to buy more. You'll wear a cute little outfit, like the ones you saw coming in here, and you'll have a lot of fun. It's inspired."

It's stupid. And it hit a little too close to home. How in the world could the disapproving daughter of an exotic dancer look herself in the eye after a night of shoving cleavage in patrons' faces in order to sell more beer? The half-floozy part of her would have a field day with this job.

Jen did not belong here.

After the interview, she stopped by a couple traditional microbreweries to inquire about job availability. It was always the same. *Leave your résumé. We'll be in touch if something opens up.*

In other words, *no.*

Her current options were to take the job Gretchen offered an hour ago or return to Washington and bartend for Mick while she weathered the storm that was her mother and waited for another brewmaster job to appear. Both options were frustrating, not to mention invitations for sexual harassment. Although at Mick's she could dress in a turtleneck and baggy jeans, cutting down on the crudeness.

At this point, nothing was going to be ideal. Ideal had been the microbrewery she planned with Chad, but she'd taken herself out of that equation. Rather, she let her mother chase her away. Again.

Frustrated, Jen drove around the streets she used to love, looking for old haunts and wondering about old friends, but there was little enjoyment in it—so much had changed. Even if it hadn't, she was no longer certain she could be comfortable here. Too many memories. Gloria had caused an uproar when her flirting at graduation turned into a full-on affair that broke up Professor Krem's thirty-year marriage and ended up with Jen cut off from the man who'd been her brewing mentor. Embarrassment had never been something Jen handled well, so she didn't keep in touch with most people who knew the story; only Mara survived the cut. Thank, God. She had no idea where she'd be without her best friend.

She wished Mara was here now, because Colorado looked and felt colder the longer she stayed. Her mother might not be here, but Mara and Chad weren't here, either.

It wasn't a fair trade.

By the time Jen rolled into the hotel parking lot, she knew … she may have found her freedom in Colorado, but it was no longer her future. And her heart?

She'd left that in Emerald Springs.

• • •

Chad slipped the sanitized tubing into the brown bottle and watched the honey-colored liquid drain from the fermentation jug. There was something Zen-like about brewing beer. When he filled the last bottle, he capped them all and carried them to the store room.

When he was done with that, reality crept back in.

Results of the fire investigation were near. Even if he hadn't heard it from Jacob when they'd crossed paths at the bakery, he'd have known the news was looming—he could feel it in his bones. He couldn't eat. He couldn't sleep.

Then again, that could just be missing Jen.

And wallowing wouldn't do. She'd made her choice. Now, he had to make a choice, too. He could whine away the rest of his life because she wasn't strong enough to see this through, or he could get up, move on, and fight for his microbrewery.

Like a sign from heaven, his phone rang, showing Dad on the display.

The report was in.

Fifteen minutes later, Chad was sitting around a meeting table flanked by Daniel and Adam with Dad at the helm.

"They don't know what caused it," Dad said.

Confusion wrinkled Chad's brow and he leaned forward in his chair. "What do you mean they don't know? They took an awful long time to say they don't know."

"There are utility connections in that room, and they believe oil in storage acted as an accelerant, but they didn't find anything criminal like gasoline or lighter fluid. The investigation will remain open. They did say beyond a reasonable doubt that the fire didn't originate in the dryer—something about burn patterns."

"That's good," Daniel said, slapping a hand to Chad's upper back.

It was, and it wasn't.

"But it still could've been arson … Marlon, Andie, or someone else," Adam said, voicing Chad's next thought.

Lately there'd been a lot of near misses around the farm and Whitman properties: anonymous calls to the IRS and INS, resulting in probes into farm business; the fence between Whitman land and Split Acres was destroyed; and now this fire. It made a man sit up and take notice.

Dad shook his head. "Marlon was passed out drunk at The Rusty Tap until closing, and then he was driven home by a friend. Andie supposedly has a pretty tight alibi, too. She was at the party, and then she went home to her little one and watched a movie. She could've snuck out after the child fell asleep, but the authorities don't seem concerned."

This was a bigger mess now than when Chad thought the blame rested on him. Andie might be a little overzealous when it came to him, but she wasn't a bad mother. She fought tooth and nail for Ava. He couldn't imagine her risking the little girl's safety by leaving her alone in order to burn down the diner to get back at him.

"What happens now?" Chad asked.

"Now we move on," Dad said. "We move on, and we stay vigilant."

Adam strummed his fingers on the table. "What about Andie? You can't expect Chad to feel comfortable around her after all this."

He got himself into this mess; he should be the one to get himself out. "According to the fire inspector, she's innocent. I can't fire her simply because I'm uncomfortable. I offered her that job in the first place—knowing our history. Besides, she needs that job."

"Send her to me," Daniel offered. "The resort has a bigger staff and a set hierarchy. She'll be paid well but put on a short leash."

Adam shook his head like he wasn't entirely on board with the idea. Chad wasn't surprised. His oldest brother's sense of integrity pushed him to walk a pretty straight line.

"Thanks, Dan," Chad said. "That sounds good, but let me talk to her first. If I get a sense she's going to make trouble for you, I'll come up with a better plan."

It was the responsible thing to do—not pass along a troubled employee simply because it was easier. Surprisingly, Chad didn't flinch at the unpleasant task ahead of him. For the first time since agreeing to run the diner, he actually saw the responsibility as a privilege rather than a curse.

Dad nodded. He looked pleased, and that further bolstered Chad's mood.

"So … we have a microbrewery to build, gentlemen." Dad's smile was infectious.

Until Chad remembered he didn't have the brewmaster.

"You done yet?" Uncle Sam poked his head into the room. "We have a deadline for those product labels. If you want to give input, Daniel, it's now or never."

Dad motioned for Daniel to leave, while Adam tagged along for "the experience."

That left Chad and Dad alone.

"Son … " Dad set his elbows on the table and his chin to his folded hands.

Right about now, a business lecture would be good because if this meeting fell apart, the only alternative was to drive home with the speedometer needle buried, trying to outrun thoughts of Jen.

"We're going to need to hire a brewmaster."

Great. So much for outrunning thoughts of Jen.

"Unless you think you can change her mind." Dad's gray brows bobbed, like convincing her to take the job was an exciting challenge. Of course he would think that—he hadn't witnessed the scene at Chad's place.

"That's not going to happen," he said.

Dad made a sound of consideration and settled back in his chair. "Because of the job in Colorado? I take it she's very close with her family."

Sure, if close meant keeping them a few states away. "She only has her mother," he said, hoping it was truthful yet evasive enough to keep his emotions level.

"And her mother is in Colorado?"

Smoothing his palm over his mouth, Chad debated the wisdom of coming clean. What would it hurt if Dad knew the truth? It wasn't like either of them would see Jen again.

"No, as far as I know, her mother is in Seattle."

Dad's eyes widened. "That's odd."

"Not really." On an exhale, Chad let it fly. "Her mother's a mess. From what I could gather, she's a first-class manipulator who lives off rich guys."

Dad's eyes widened even further. "Interesting."

"And Jen thinks if she stays here she's putting us at risk, especially after she heard about my past track record."

"Suddenly it all makes sense, doesn't it?" Dad replied.

He clenched his fists in frustration as they set atop the table. "Not really. I don't see why she doesn't just tell the woman to stay away."

"Like Zoe tells Marlon to stay away. You see how that works."

Yeah. Lately Marlon had been like a ticking time bomb, causing trouble all over the place. It was impossible for Zoe to live without some drama.

"Handling Marlon became a lot easier once we all got involved, wouldn't you say?"

He nodded slowly. "Yeah. He still causes trouble, but it's contained because we expect him to cause trouble."

"Exactly. It's hard to be taken by surprise when everyone knows it's going to happen."

Had Jen ever tried to neutralize the situation with her mother by warning people? Probably not. She wanted to handle everything on her own. Heck, she only told him out of desperation after he saw the text messages and pushed for an answer.

Dad smacked his palms on the table. "Now, back to the reason I kept you here. We need to hire a brewmaster. Do you know any?"

"I do," Chad said, pushing to stand because now he had an idea to keep Gloria Chavez in check.

He just hoped to God it was enough to convince Jen to give him and the microbrewery another chance.

Chapter Eighteen

Walking into the lobby of Four Seasons, Jen filled with doubt. The handful of times she'd made half-hearted attempts to reason with her mother over the years always led to more heartache. *I do it for you, baby. How else are we going to survive?*

But lots of women raised children on their own in non-toxic atmospheres. And the way Jen operated, sprinting away from everything good to protect it from bad, wasn't survival. On the contrary, it was wearing her down. If she didn't do something to stop the vicious cycle, she was going to end up destroying herself.

Enough was enough.

There was power in a decision like that.

Her phone rang. *Chad.* Twice in ten minutes. If she was anywhere but here, she'd answer.

After the scene in his driveway, she was surprised he was calling. A little nugget of hope lodged beneath her breast. She didn't have the right to dream he wanted her back—especially not before she settled things with her mother.

With a lump in her throat, she sent the call to voicemail and powered across the shiny stone floor toward the lounge.

Jen couldn't remember ever initiating a meeting with her mother. She'd spent her whole life hiding from her.

"Baby girl," squealed the made-up woman in a tight red dress as she slipped off a barstool.

A few afternoon patrons took in the ruckus. There was always a scene with Gloria around.

Tired from the trip to Colorado and home again, Jen's patience was thin.

The bartender grinned like he was in on some joke, and that made Jen think Gloria had been flirting. She didn't need some pretty boy, man candy coming to Gloria's rescue if the conversation turned ugly, so Jen motioned to a table across the room.

"Can we sit?" she asked, evading a hug by not waiting for a reply.

"Don't you want anything from the bar?" Mom asked as she clip-clopped behind Jen.

She wanted a lot of things, but alcohol wasn't one of them—unless it was beer she brewed … in Emerald Springs.

"Nope," Jen said. "I just want to talk."

Her phone vibrated again, and she glanced at the incoming text on the screen as she sat.

All systems go on the microbrewery. PLEASE don't take that job without talking to me.

Her heart stuttered. Chad's text could only mean one thing. If she handled her mother effectively, she could have everything she wanted. The microbrewery … and him.

Talk about pressure.

Jen typed a hasty K and focused on the task at hand.

"I'm so glad you called," Mom said. "I've wanted you to meet Raj."

Before Jen could process the change of topic, Mom stood, gesturing to the entrance.

No, no, no, no, no.

Raj was a little man with a sweet smile and a gaudy fashion sense. He wore an ascot. Under different circumstances, Jen would've made some kind of joke.

A full foot taller, Gloria rushed to his side and kissed his balding head.

Jen was embarrassed enough already. She did not want to have this conversation with an audience—especially one that consisted of a man Gloria was bilking.

"*This* is my daughter."

The man held a hand to his stomach and offered a little bow as greeting.

Jen swallowed her pride and smiled.

"You're every bit as beautiful as your mother," he said.

Even though Raj's compliment seemed harmless, it made Jen squirm. That kind of observation, usually accompanied by unprovoked leers, made her feel dirty as a child. As an adult who didn't respect her mother, the comparison didn't feel much better.

As if she expected the resistance, Gloria jumped in, distracting Raj, saving Jen from acknowledging his compliment. "Honey, can I get you a drink?" she cooed as she hung on his arm.

He marveled at her. "No. I'm going to make a few business calls. You ladies enjoy your time together." He smiled at Jen. "It was my pleasure. Enjoy yourself. The fun's on me." He patted his breast pocket and turned away.

Staring after him as he waddled toward the door, Jen took shallow breaths. He seemed … decent. Not anywhere near as slimy as the gold-chain wearing guy on the boat.

"He's such a gentleman," Gloria said.

Her mother was almost swooning. If it weren't so ridiculously depressing, it would be hilariously cliché—the aging stripper with her height-challenged sugar daddy.

Squeezing her hands together beneath the table, Jen took a fortifying breath. She couldn't believe she was going to dig deeper into this "relationship," but she needed to segue into the conversation she came to have.

"How did you meet?" she asked, and then promptly choked on her tongue.

"We've known each other for years." Mom was sitting now, toying with the stem of her wine glass, watching the entrance wistfully. "He came into the club shortly after you were born, and he's been an angel in the background ever sense."

"Is he married?" They usually had one of two things: a wife or a criminal record. Sometimes, they had both.

Gloria laughed. "He's been married off and on over the years, but not currently. You never know. Maybe my timing is finally right."

Hmm. Jen sat back, breathing evenly. For some reason, this didn't feel as desperate and dirty as she expected it to feel—not that it couldn't sink to that level at any moment.

The thing was she hadn't prepared for this. In a way, she was now almost rooting for her mother.

She should've known this wouldn't be easy. It never had been. *Blurred lines.* At the crux of it all was this woman who gave Jen life and kept her fed. It was the minimum, but it counted for something, didn't it?

The words Jen came to say sounded harsh in her head. *You embarrass me.* At the moment, the only thing embarrassing about Gloria was the obscene amount of cleavage revealed by the skintight dress.

You embarrass me. Jen tried the words again. They still didn't match with the woman sipping Chardonnay wearing a peaceful expression. Who was this woman? Not the woman Jen remembered. That woman had been an exotic dancer, a kept woman, and a mistress. None of it was particularly pride-inducing, but those things weren't exactly illegal. Jen had assumed Mom couldn't be trusted because many a scorned wife had shown up at their ratty apartment door shouting as much—and worse. It was from these women that Jen learned words like *prostitute* and *whore*, and heard for the first time that her mother was a thief. Little by little, Jen believed them. It seemed more rational than the idea men gave their money away willingly or with no strings attached.

But what if those women lied, too? What if Mom never stole a dime? Did that change anything?

With an elbow propped on the table, Jen nibbled on her fingernail. Maybe it did change some things, though at the moment, she couldn't name any. All she knew was, it didn't change one thing: Jen still didn't want Mom prowling around the Whitmans.

She pushed on. "Remember the check you saw in my living room?"

Mom grinned. "The one with the personal note?"

She nodded, feeling less and less sure with every passing moment. "The Whitmans have offered me a job brewing beer in a microbrewery they're building."

"How exciting!" Mom's eyes widened, and Jen hoped it wasn't because she was seeing dollar signs.

"It is exciting," Jen continued, filled with heavy dread. "But I turned it down."

Mom gasped. "Why?"

"Because of you." Her mouth felt tacky as she watched her mother's facial features twist.

"Because of me? Why?"

This was the most communication she'd had with her mother since she left Miami. Her throbbing heart, low-grade headache, and clammy hands made it about as pleasant as a root canal. But she had to get through it if she wanted to get past it.

"I was afraid," Jen said. And she still was, but for a different reason. What if the situation with Mom wasn't as bad as it seemed? What if embarrassment was really the most Jen had to fear?

She would've lost Chad and the microbrewery for no good reason.

"What were you afraid of?" Mom asked.

The longer Jen sat here, pushing words from her mouth, the more fresh air reached the closed-up parts of her heart. It was compelling, so she opened wide and continued. "I was afraid of you embarrassing me, like you did at graduation."

Gloria's brow furrowed. "I told you I was sorry about that. He'd told me he was separated."

Jen cringed at the reminder. "I know, but after that, all the pictures, the men, and the comments about me needing to latch onto a man with money in order to survive. It became a constant reminder of what happened at graduation, what happened my whole childhood, and how it could happen again. Any man was fair game. Not just a married man, but a man who meant something to me." Jen swallowed. "Do you know he never talked to me again?" He'd been the closest thing she'd had to a father. "Your lifestyle … hurts me. And I'm not going to let it hurt me anymore. I'd rather walk away from you for good than walk away from a shot at a stable and happy life."

Mom's shoulders drooped, but then she shrugged. Staring at her wine glass, she offered a sad, little smile. "You know? I'm oddly happy you feel that way." She looked up, her brown eyes piercing through Jen. "It means your life should be a lot easier than mine, because you won't be trapped in a vicious cycle of poverty and self-hatred. It's an awful place to be. Do I have regrets? You bet I do. But anything I did to keep you alive and with me isn't one of them. Look at you. Despite my example, you're strong, college educated, and successful. You're everything I could only dream of being. I'm so proud of you, and I'm sorry."

Years of embarrassment and resentment broke free like a calving glacier, causing a rush of tears. The words didn't make all of the actions right, but hearing them at this juncture somehow softened the memories that had been driving Jen.

In an action she couldn't have fathomed an hour ago, Jen reached across the table and took her mother's hand. "I know," she said, sniffing to maintain composure. "I just wanted a better life for both of us."

Mom patted her free hand atop Jen's. "Well, now you know how I feel."

• • •

Chad stared at the one-letter text from Jen.

K

What the hell did that mean?

When he called, she refused to answer her phone, and when he sent a text all she gave him in return was one letter.

What was he supposed to do with that?

Stilling at his desk inside the empty diner, Chad tried to be happy, but he couldn't quite believe Jen's *K* meant *Fine. I will talk to you because I'm open to another chance.* If that were the case, wouldn't she have typed more than a single letter? Maybe *K* meant, *Yeah, right, whatever, Chad. I'm done with you.*

He didn't feel she meant that either.

Four hours had passed since he received her one-letter text. If he wasn't reading too hard into it, he would've texted her back by now. Instead, he sat here stewing.

He hadn't been privy to her Colorado trip itinerary, so he'd tried to give her the benefit of the doubt—maybe she was in the air. He glanced at the time on his laptop. In his anxiousness, he may have looked up the flight time. Denver to Seattle was under three hours. Surely, whatever *K* meant could've been expanded upon by now—*four hours later.*

He growled.

"Hey."

Chad looked up to see a somber-faced Andie in the doorway. "Hey." He motioned for her to come in.

She started to close the door but then shrugged. "Guess that's not necessary anymore."

With the diner closed during repairs to the fire-damaged room, there was no one to overhear their meeting, which was good. He wasn't sure what to expect. Andie contacted him, initiating this meeting before he got a chance to call her.

"Thanks for meeting with me," she said, looking more nervous than usual, keeping a good distance between them.

He supposed that was bound to happen after the authorities questioned her about the fire. Being accused of arson wasn't a unifying event.

Chad nodded. "I've been meaning to talk to you, too."

She folded her arms across her chest and exhaled. "I quit."

He blinked. His mouth opened as if there were words to be said, but his brain stuttered. He was pretty sure he knew why she was quitting, and it was the right thing to do, but he was surprised, nonetheless. If she didn't have Ava, he wouldn't be worried.

"We're going to head back to my mom's in Iowa."

"Do you have a job waiting for you?"

She shook her head. "No, but I have some connections, and I'm thinking about going back to school." Her nose wrinkled. "Don't worry. I'm not going to ask you for a letter of recommendation or to be a reference or anything."

That was the right thing to do, too. He wouldn't lie for her. Even cleared of any wrongdoing as far as the fire was concerned, he couldn't overlook her breeches in professional conduct.

"I didn't start that fire," she said. "Ava means more to me than you ever did."

There was a little more venom than necessary in her statement.

"I know," he said, satisfied with her reasoning but refusing to be dragged into a more personal conversation. She was a resigning employee, and he was her manager. In the time she'd been working here, he never once lost sight of those boundaries.

It wasn't his fault she did.

"Good luck to you," he said, meaning every word.

"Good luck with *this* place," she said with a touch of sarcasm in her wish.

He didn't need luck to get this place up and running. He had money and determination to spare.

But he sure could use a little luck with Jen.

Chapter Nineteen

Jen sat on the end of her bed, staring at her phone. What if she texted or called Chad only to find out his message was something negative?

She groaned. Why was she doing this to herself? Didn't talking to Mom teach her anything?

Yes, it did. Fear was usually blown way out of proportion.

Sucking a breath through her open mouth, Jen typed I'm, but deleted it as quickly as it appeared.

I'm an idiot. Obviously. Because she was stuck on the end of this bed worried a man who said he loved her a few days ago had suddenly changed his mind. She might not know a lot about love, but she knew it wasn't here today, gone tomorrow.

Mara stuck her head into the room. "We're headed out." She studied Jen, and her face wrinkled. "Mick … " she called over her shoulder, "give me a sec."

"No, go."

"No way." She sat on the corner of the bed. "Not until you look like you're mentally stable enough to leave alone."

Jen nudged her with her shoulder. "I'm fine."

"Fine shouldn't look like you're a get-drunk-and-pass-out risk." Mara glanced at the phone in Jen's hand. "What did he say?"

"Nothing since the last text telling me not to take the Colorado job until I talk to him."

"What did you say?"

"K."

Mara sighed. "That's it? Jen, he wants you to talk to him. You need to say more than K."

"What if he has something bad to say?"

"Like what?"

Jen slumped, her body folding in around her heart. "I don't know. Like … he doesn't love me anymore and he wants me to stay away." After she jumped ship on him, maybe she deserved it.

"Do you think that makes sense?" Mara grabbed the phone. "Honey, he wrote 'please' in all caps. That's begging."

It was, wasn't it?

"Call him," Mara said, giving Jen back the phone and gripping her arm. "I'll stay right here for moral support. I'll even hold your hand."

Something in Mara's generous but pathetic offer kicked Jen in the ass, lifting her off the bed with a huff. "What am I doing?"

"Going to the bathroom?" Mara asked.

"It was rhetorical."

Mara laughed.

Jen crossed the room, grabbing her overnight bag. She wasn't going to call Chad. She was going to see him. She'd been gutsy enough to tell him in person she was leaving. She could be gutsy enough to tell him in person she wanted another chance.

"That a girl," Mara said. "I'll help you pack."

"I'm not assuming he's going to want me to stay," Jen said. The need to rationalize her behavior was strong ever since her meeting with Mom. Maybe things could've been better between them sooner had Jen been honest with her feelings from the beginning.

"Okay," Mara said.

"I'm just emotionally drained and physically whipped from the flight. It would be dangerous for me to turn around and drive back to Seattle."

Mara smiled and slipped an arm around Jen's shoulder. "He's going to ask you to stay."

Her exhale was broken. *God, she hoped so.* She'd never wanted anything more than she wanted this.

As she drove, Jen contemplated calling him, telling him she was on her way, but the idea he might tell her to turn around kept her eyes on the road and her phone in the center console. He'd have a much harder time turning her down when they were face to face.

The more she drove, the more her nerves settled. There was something about the monotony of the highway that soothed her. She'd faced a lot of insurmountable odds and ugly things in her life. Facing Chad under any circumstances didn't compare to those.

Over the past month, she'd softened somehow, opened up to people and places she never imagined she would, but she was still strong and determined—more so than she ever knew. Twice today she'd run toward people and situations she would've run away from a month ago.

The sense of empowerment was thrilling.

She might've been born—beyond her control—the daughter of Gloria and Ricardo Chavez into a world where she was mostly an afterthought, but she raised herself to be more than that. She wasn't half-floozy, half-deadbeat, like she'd always assumed. She'd been giving them too much credit. Maybe an eighth each was all they deserved.

That meant Jen Chavez was seventy-five percent whatever she wanted to be.

Adjusting her grip on the wheel as she glimpsed the Welcome to Emerald Springs sign, Jen smiled. She wanted to be the world's best brewmaster and the woman Chad Whitman loved.

• • •

Chad couldn't take Jen's silence anymore. He gave her until he reached his front porch to reply, and when she didn't, he decided to get to the bottom of whatever the hell was going on.

Do you have any idea when you might be ready to talk to me?

He typed, hoping the text didn't read as desperate as he felt.

He stared at the phone. The screen didn't change. This was bullshit.

Walking into his bedroom, he belly flopped on the bed. Maybe it was time to face the truth—K had meant kiss-off.

Damn it. He pushed to sit.

The phone vibrated.

I'm ready now.

Relief softened his muscles as his thumb hovered above her name, ready to call and hear her voice, but before he could hit the button the doorbell rang.

Whoever it was had terrible timing.

Give me a second, he typed, hoping the delay wouldn't set them back to the point where Jen started using K again.

"Coming," he called to the intruder, pledging to have the person gone in five seconds flat.

But one foot inside the living room with a clear shot to the screen door, he realized he never wanted the person standing on his porch to leave him again.

"Hi," Jen said, offering a weak wave and an even weaker smile. She held up her phone.

He took her in, from the tips of her sexy, black ankle boots to the silky top of her head. Her tan skin looked sallow, and her wide eyes hazy, but still she was the most beautiful thing he'd ever seen.

Maybe it was a mirage. Maybe he wanted to hear from her so badly he'd caused a break with reality. He released a loaded exhale.

"Do you want me to go?" she stuttered, taking one step back.

"God, no." He shook off the shock and rushed the door. "I'm just … surprised."

She nodded, wringing her hands at her belted waist. "I thought you liked surprises."

He pushed against the screen, opening the door. "I do. Normally. But last time … "

"Was a mistake," she said, stepping toward him, sweeping her tongue across her lips. "I should've handled that better. I'm sorry. If I had it to do over again, I would do it differently."

She was inches away, looking up at him with her lips parted and wide, her eyes, shiny. It was a breathtaking expression of anticipation and sincerity.

Chad could no longer keep his hands to himself. Raising a palm to her soft, warm cheek, he stepped even closer.

"You're here now," he whispered. "So how 'bout I give you a 'do over'?"

Her lashes fluttered. "You'd do that for me?"

Using his back to hold open the door, he lifted his other hand, threading it through her hair. "I'd do anything for you."

He kissed her sweetly, parting his lips for a tiny taste. He breathed her in, held her close, and made a silent vow. As long as she wanted him, he was hers.

She surprised him with a shove to his chest, and then she was down the steps, striding over the gravel toward her car.

"Hey, where are you going?" he asked.

"I want my 'do over.'" She threw him a smile as she assumed the same position he'd found her in that awful day she went away. "Now, run to me."

He chuckled. "Run to you?"

"Yeah, you jogged to me last time, and then you hugged me."

Grinning, he hopped off the porch. "I can handle that."

When he wrapped her in his arms and lifted off the ground, she laughed. "Now, tell me you like surprises."

"I like surprises," he said.

"I love you, too."

Jen's arms wound around his waist and she rested her head atop his heart. Her words echoed on the breeze as he held her close, stroking her hair, so damn grateful for the chance to get this right.

"You do?" he asked, keeping the conversation alive. Maybe he just wanted to work around to her saying it again.

She looked at him. "I do."

"And that's why you came back?"

She nodded. "Yep. It hurt too much to imagine loving you while I was hundreds of miles away."

Thank God she'd seen how senseless it was to find someone who lit up your life only to have to learn to live without them. Brushing his lips across her forehead, he relaxed, waiting for his heartbeat to settle and the blanket of goose bumps to disappear.

"What about your mom?" he asked, the fear Jen would run again just beneath the surface.

"I talked to her, and I'm trying to be more rational where she's concerned." Her face wrinkled. "But I still don't want her sitting next to your dad at dinner."

Chad chuckled. "We'll sit her beside Dan instead. He's pretty much immune to smooth-talking women."

Jen indulged in a little laugh, but it quickly faded. "What did the inspector find?"

"Nothing really. The investigation was inconclusive, but it ruled out Marlon, Andie … and me." He smiled. "Beyond a shadow of a doubt they said it wasn't me."

"I never thought it was."

"You're biased."

She sighed and lifted her lips to his. "I totally am."

This kiss lasted longer than the first, giving him time to enjoy her warm weight against his chest. As he angled his head for a better vantage point of her mouth, he knew he could stay like this forever.

His life would be lacking without Jen Chavez to kiss.

This time, when she shoved him away, she walked toward the house, grinning an invitation. This surprise visit was turning out to be so much better than her last.

He jogged onto the porch and opened the screen door. He'd never paid much attention to this place. It had a roof, a bathroom, and a bed. That was pretty much all he cared about. But with Jen standing in the middle of the living room, he saw his past, his future, and everything in between.

Complete contentment grabbed hold of his overheated body, leaving him with a good dose of chills.

"So what comes next?" she asked, spinning around to face him.

"You should probably marry me." His eyes widened at the spontaneous words.

Jen gaped. "Wow. I wasn't expecting to hear that."

He gave a nervous chuckle. "I wasn't expecting to say it, either." He shrugged. "But, you know, I'm glad I did, because it makes perfect sense."

"You think?" There was a sparkle in her eye and an inquisitive hitch to her brow.

"I do." He grinned. "I mean I love you. You love me." He walked to her. "And then there's that matter of my little rule."

She wound her arms around his neck. "What rule?"

"I don't date employees.

"Somebody told me about that rule."

"The good news is I never said I couldn't marry one."

She laughed, lighting off tiny fireworks beneath his skin with the sound. "Smooth—real smooth."

The way his smile dug into his face, the expression had to be permanent. "So what do you say? Will you marry me and brew my beer?"

Jen stared at him for the longest time—long enough to give him a nervous twinge—and then she grinned. "Yeah. I'll marry you, but it'll be *our* beer, and I won't be your employee anymore, because I'll be your *partner*. Fifty-fifty split, baby. Outside the brew house, of course. I call the shots in there."

"Oh yeah?" He gathered her up in his arms, walking backward toward the bedroom. "Then it's only fair I call the shots in here."

"Fat chance, buddy," she squealed as he nibbled on her exposed shoulder.

He'd say his odds were much better than *fat*. He got the microbrewery. He got the girl.

He couldn't image anything luckier than that.

About the Author

Elley Arden is a born and bred Pennsylvanian who has lived as far west as Utah and as far north as Wisconsin. She drinks wine like it's water (a slight exaggeration), prefers a night at the ballpark to a night on the town, and believes almond English toffee is the key to happiness. Elley writes contemporary romances for Crimson Romance. For a complete list of Elley's books, visit *www.elleyarden.com*.

A Sneak Peek from Emerald Springs Legacy Book Four
(From *Daniel's Decision* by Nicole Flockton)

Daniel Whitman swirled the glass tumbler, watching the amber liquid circle and cling to the outer edges of the glass, the ice clinking against the sides in musical accompaniment. It did little to drown out the rest of the noise coming from the party going on behind him.

He should be celebrating with the rest of his family. He was happy his little brother had found contentment and happiness in his life. Jen, his brother's brand new fiancée, had made remarkable changes to his wayward, fun-loving younger brother in a few short weeks. Seems everyone around him was finding love—including his father. He took another gulp and welcomed the burn of the malt whiskey down his throat.

What he felt like doing was buying a bottle of the twenty-year-old whiskey he was drinking and having his own private little party. Instead he lifted his near empty glass in a signal to the barman that he wanted a top up.

"Everything all right, son?" his father asked as he slipped onto the empty barstool next to him.

Dan raised his almost empty glass in a mock salute. "Absolutely, just having a quiet drink."

"You might want to go easy on that," Richard Whitman said as he inclined his head at the glass in Dan's hand.

He let out a harsh laugh and downed the rest of the contents of his glass before he spoke to his father. "It's my first drink, Dad."

He felt rather than heard the heavy sigh his father let out. "Look, you're still not upset about the meeting this afternoon, are you? You know Adam and I thought long and hard about your expansion plans for the resort. We agree they have merit and will be a good idea in the future, but with the new microbrewery, we can't justify another large capital outlay. "

Daniel loved his older brother, Adam. He had missed him while Adam was away carving out his own career in Los Angeles. But during that time Dan and his father had grown close and discussed business ideas. Now with Adam back, it was like Richard disregarded all those discussions and now listened to only Adam. He knew it had bothered Chad too, but Chad had eventually talked them around. Maybe he could use this opportunity to plant the seed in Richard's mind that proceeding now with the plans for the resort was the way to go.

"You do realize, Dad, we are missing out on a niche market? When we had actor Michael Williams staying at the resort, he loved the privacy we afforded him. It was the first time in years he and his wife had been able to have a vacation where no paparazzi bothered them. Where they didn't have to worry about pictures of them in compromising positions appearing in the press." Daniel warmed to his topic and his earlier melancholy mood drifted away on the breeze. "Look, Dad, if we added a few high-class facilities to the ones we already have, and increase the services we offer in the spa, get something that is totally unique to our resort, I believe we'd be running at nearly full capacity all year round. Not to mention a few other changes to our processes and we could be totally eco- and environmentally friendly. Those sort of features appeal to the rich and famous."

"Son, these changes you're proposing don't sound cheap. How can you guarantee that if we lay out all this money, we will run at capacity? It's a big risk and at present it's one I'm not prepared to take, especially as we have the new microbrewery expansion." Richard paused and picked up the drink the bartender had placed in front of him. "Besides, how do you propose we attract these *high-class* guests to the resort? If we publicize our products and services, we effectively neutralize our anonymity, which according to you, is the main drawing card for these guests."

"Word of mouth, Dad. I told Michael we were looking at making changes, and he said to let him know when we did. He'd come back and let all his friends know."

"That was a bit presumptuous of you, wasn't it? Son, I know I gave control of the resort to you, but the final decision is still mine."

Dan bit back the groan of frustration that threatened to burst out of him. Why couldn't his father see what a great business decision this was? He'd worked up a business plan, worked out all the costs of making the necessary changes to make the resort one hundred percent eco-friendly. There wasn't a lot more they had to do to make the changes. And with Adam's knowledge, it would be so easy. The main backbone of his father's business had been organic—sheesh, his dad knew Chad's microbrewery was going to be organic. The resort had been one of the first to use the latest technology in green energy. They treated him like he didn't know how to do anything. He had an MBA in business, for heavens sake. He couldn't understand why his father was not keen to proceed with the plans he'd presented that afternoon.

"Look, Dad, we already have a good reputation as a resort that uses green energy, but we're getting a little tired. We need to freshen things up, offer new and innovative spa techniques. I can't say it enough: I want to draw a different crowd to the resort." Daniel plunged ahead with an idea he hadn't presented that afternoon to his father and brothers. "In addition to trying to find something new and innovative to the resort, I'm also looking at introducing holistic massages and treatments to help with the treatment of cancer. Mom would've loved this. She'd have been helping me research it all."

He closed his eyes and let the memories of his mom wash over him. Even after five years he still missed her like crazy. He must have been the only kid in his school whose mom had been his best friend. Sheila Whitman had always had time for him—no matter how busy she was she'd stop and sit with him. Listen to him. Encourage him. She always believed in him. Always thought his ideas were fantastic. She had been his biggest champion.

God, he wished she was here right now. She'd be able to talk his dad around and convince his father that Dan's plans were exactly what the resort needed.

"Yes, I'm sure she would've loved that. She always believed that eating the organic fruit from the farm slowed her illness." His father's words were quiet and filled with admiration for the woman who'd tried with all her might to fight the insidious disease that had taken hold of her and had never let her go.

Daniel nodded and took another sip of the whiskey, not needing the numbing sensation he had craved a half an hour ago. "There have been great leaps in the introduction of holistic treatments in helping cancer patients recover from chemotherapy and radiation sessions. A lot of new techniques have been introduced to people's cancer treatment plans, ranging from massages to herbal teas to acupuncture to diet changes, including eating totally organic produce. We have a chance to reach that market, too. The possibilities are endless, Dad, surely you can see that."

"Dan, I can't argue with anything you're saying. Out of all my sons you've been the one with the business acumen. You have ensured the resort has always been profitable, and I couldn't be prouder of you. However, we just can't do it at the moment. Maybe in a year's time."

"In a year's time it will be too late. Already other resorts are starting to make these changes. There's a resort in Australia that is a leader in the market. I've been trying to speak to their marketing manager but haven't had any luck yet. I thought about taking a trip down there to check it out."

"That's a long way to go. Surely there are other resorts in the United States that will give you everything you need."

"You've seen all the research I presented to you earlier. This is a world-class resort and we could learn a lot from them."

"Richard, darling, are you ready to go?"

Daniel gripped his glass a little tighter as a new person entered their conversation. He still found it hard to believe his father and their housekeeper, Patty, were now an item. The idea seemed so foreign to him. His father loving another woman. A woman who wasn't his mother.

He kept his eyes focused on his hands and not on what he was sure would be Patty touching his father's arm.

"Give me a couple more minutes, sweetheart, then I'll be ready to go."

Dan tried not to flinch when he heard the sound of lips meeting in a quick kiss. He needed to get out of there. There was no point continuing with the conversation. It was a dead-end. He placed his glass back on the bar, pulled a couple of bills out of his wallet, and threw them down.

"It's okay, Dad, I'm leaving now anyway." He couldn't deny the happiness shining out of his father's face. It didn't mean he had to like it though. "I'll see you both later."

He turned and walked away, not bothering to say goodbye to his brothers. He was sure they'd give him hell over it later, but at the moment he didn't care. He just needed to get away.

The cool night air hit him and he welcomed its freshness. He'd walked to the restaurant, as he knew he'd probably have a few drinks and it wouldn't be a good idea for him to drive home. He'd been right. He used the time to clear his head and work out what his next move would be.

There were so many changes happening around him. Both of his brothers were now engaged. His father was in love with his housekeeper. Even Colleen, the daughter of his father's former business partner, had fallen in love and was expecting a baby. She'd been the last person he, and everyone else in town, had expected to succumb to Cupid's clutches. It appeared there was something in the water in Emerald Springs and he planned to stay as far away from it as possible. The very idea of falling in love and getting married was an anathema to him. He'd loved his mother, and when she'd died it had been so hard for him to feel anything. He couldn't imagine letting himself be vulnerable like that again, to lay his heart on the line and give it to someone to look after. There was no guarantee they wouldn't tread on it, and he'd have to pick the pieces up again. There would definitely be no trip down the aisle in his foreseeable future.

He reached the front door of his house as his phone rang. He pulled it out of his pocket along with his keys and glanced at the caller idea as he unlocked the door.

Adam.

The last thing he wanted was to talk to his brother. But he knew if he didn't answer it, both his brothers would be camped on his doorstep first thing in the morning.

"Hey, Adam, what's up?"

"You tell me, Dan. You left Chad and Jen's engagement celebration dinner without saying goodbye. That's not like you, so what gives?"

Dan closed his door and walked down the hallway, his footsteps echoing around him. His house seemed quiet and lonely.

"Nothing, man, I'm just tired."

Even to his own ears he didn't sound convincing, and there was no way Adam was going to let him get away with it.

"I saw you talking to Dad. Tell me you're not still annoyed about the resort plans. It's just not—"

"I know, I know, it's just not good timing," he interrupted his brother. "I heard it from Dad again tonight. The fact that you guys can't see how this will improve the overall profit of the organization baffles me. You both have made your decision, but it doesn't mean I have to agree with it or like it or even follow it."

"What have you got planned, little brother?" Suspicion laced Adam's every word.

"Nothing," Dan sighed and ran his fingers through his hair. He wanted off the phone. "Nothing at all. Look I need to go. I'll speak to you later. Bye."

Adam's answering goodbye faded as he pulled the phone away from his ear. He tossed it and his keys onto the coffee table in his lounge room, right on top of the plans he'd shown to his family this afternoon. He sat down on the couch and picked them up. Every time he looked at them, he got excited. The possibilities were endless.

His phone buzzed for a second time and he knew who it would be without having to check caller ID. He picked it up and connected the call.

"Hey, Chad, I'm fine."

His younger brother's chuckle drifted down the line. "I should be mad at you for slinking out on me. I had so much more fun planned for you. One of Jen's friends was eyeing you earlier. Seems she likes the brooding, silent, suit type. Guess there's no accounting for taste."

"Bro, I *don't* need you to do any matchmaking, thanks. I can find my own dates; I've never had to rely on you or Adam to set me up."

"What about Becky and her sister, Trina?"

Dan burst out laughing. He could always count on Chad to lighten his mood. "Man, that was the date from hell and besides, you tricked me into going with you."

"Who knew Trina was an octopus in disguise?"

Dan recalled how Trina's hands seemed to have a life of their own—all over his body. "Well I don't plan on falling into the trap you and Adam have fallen into. I've got my life planned out and getting married isn't even listed among the pages at present."

"Famous last words, bro, famous last words. Careful, it's contagious you know. Even the old man's got hit."

Just like that, Dan's good mood evaporated. He didn't need any reminders about his father and Patty. "Yeah well, not happening here. I've got too much to do before I'd even consider entering into a serious relationship with someone."

Dan glanced down at the computer that had fired up when he'd dropped his keys on the table. A picture of a stunning wooden structure surrounded by lush green trees glared out at him. A plan quickly flared to life in his brain. He wanted to get away and what better place to do that than the resort he wanted Emerald Paradise Resort to emulate? That Kulang Resort was on the other side of the world was the perfect solution to his problem with being surrounded by sickening happiness.

"Listen Chad, I'm going to take a trip. I'll probably be gone for a couple of weeks. When I get there I'll call you."

"Whoa, man, what?"

If anyone could understand his frustrations, it would be Chad. Chad had fought tooth and nail for his plans. The fact that microbrewery had put his resort on the back burner should annoy him, but he was proud of his little brother and he couldn't hold it against him.

"I need to get away, bro. I need some space to deal with everything that's happening around here. I just can't deal with seeing—"

"Okay, I get it." Chad interrupted. "Look, just let me know when you get to wherever you're going and I'll break the news to Dad and Adam that you've done a runner."

"I've not done a runner, I'm going on a scouting trip."

"The less I know, the less trouble I'll get into," Chad said on a laugh. "I got your back, Dan."

"Thanks, Chad, I owe you."

"Big time, bro. Take care."

As Chad disconnected the call, Dan opened up a search engine and typed in the website for an airline. Half an hour later he had his flights and accommodations booked. In three days he'd be in Australia inspecting Kulang Resort. He would make the changes to his resort, even if he had to use his own money.

•••

Rochelle Harris straightened the flowers on the reception desk. The perfume from the lilies was subtle but refreshing. She straightened a magazine and gave a slight nod, satisfied that the area looked neat but welcoming.

She loved her job. There was nothing more fulfilling than seeing people enter the resort tired and in desperate need of relaxation and then check out with an abundance of energy and eagerly booking their next visit to the resort. To know it was all because of her innovative marketing techniques to draw the guests in was even more satisfying.

It wasn't hard to relax, not when surrounded by luscious, healthy rainforest and treatments meant to restore a tired soul. Even she made sure she booked in for a weekly hot stone massage to ensure her energy levels were constantly on an even level.

As she gave the reception area another once over, she noticed a man walking into the resort. He strode confidently in through the doors; even she could see the self-assurance emanating from him. She pegged him as a successful businessman, and he probably had a glossy, perfectly made up woman following behind him.

Except he didn't. He didn't waver in his strides, as if he was waiting for someone to catch up with him.

She made her way a bit closer to the reception desk. It wasn't unusual but it definitely wasn't common for a single man to come to the resort. She moved behind the counter, smiling at one of the staff as she did so. She'd been known to help out with guest check-in if things were busy. It wasn't part of her job description, but it was a great way to hear what people thought of the resort. She'd come up with several ways to streamline various aspects of the resort by listening to guests.

"Good morning, sir, and welcome to Kulang Resort."

Rochelle smiled as she heard the front desk clerk greet her mystery guest. She had no idea why she was so interested in him. He'd piqued her curiosity the moment he'd walked through the door. She risked a glance at him and looked quickly away. Up close he was even more magnetic. She tried to ignore the increase in her heart rate. She wasn't normally one who liked a five o'clock shadow on a man, but on this guest it was extremely sexy.

She pushed the thought away. It was not good policy to get involved with the guests. It could be detrimental to her career. She'd made the mistake once and she wasn't going to do it again. Not to mention she wasn't going to let attraction to a man sway her from her path in life. Before she even considered getting seriously involved again, she was going to make sure she had financial security. She wasn't going to rely on anyone for the ability to purchase the things she wanted, when she wanted them.

She was on track to have a decent deposit on a house, and her share portfolio was performing rather nicely. Not bad for a girl who had to start working at fifteen in a beauty salon and then go to school part-time so she could get her marketing degree. However, that was in the past and she had carved out her own future. She was in control of her destiny and she didn't need to get distracted from that by a handsome stranger. Especially a guest of the resort.

"Good morning, my name's Daniel Whitman and I have a reservation."

Daniel Whitman.

Why did that name ring a bell? She racked her brain, trying to see if there was something that would trigger where she knew the name. He was American; she got that from his accent.

Was he a returning guest? No, she didn't think he was. But then again it wasn't like she knew all the guests who had ever stayed at the resort.

Daniel Whitman.

It was bugging her that she couldn't remember.

"I see you haven't booked in for any for the treatments the resort offers, Mr. Whitman. Is there something in particular you'd like?"

Rochelle couldn't help the smile that broke out over her face. She'd trained the staff to ensure the guests were aware of all the services the resort offered.

"I haven't made up my mind what I'd like to try, but when I do I'll let you know. Your resort has so much to offer, it's almost too hard to choose."

There was nothing in what he said that should have caused her memory to unlock, but she suddenly knew who Daniel Whitman was. He was the person who had been emailing her to get information about the resort. She'd not responded because she wasn't sure if he was legitimate. She had been too caught up with the new marketing and expansion plans she'd been working on to take time to do proper research on the resort he said he was from.

Now was the perfect opportunity to find out why he was here and what he wanted from her. If he wanted anything that is. She took a step forward and held out her hand toward him.

"Good morning, Mr. Whitman, I'm Rochelle Harris, marketing manager at Kulang Resort. You've been emailing me, right?"

Rochelle wasn't prepared for the sensations that shot through her the moment Daniel grasped her hand. It took everything in her to shake his hand professionally and not pull away and tuck it behind her back.

"Ms. Harris, finally we connect." His voice had lowered fractionally and the hint of a smile he sent her way did nothing to quell the feelings that were starting to override her good sense.

He sounded so calm, as if their hands touching didn't affect him in any way. It probably didn't; it was probably nothing new to him at all. The feelings she was experiencing were thanks her being super sensitive as to why he was here at the resort.

"I wouldn't say connect, Mr. Whitman, but welcome to the resort. I hope you enjoy your stay with us."

He looked her up and done, and she worked hard to control the slow rise of heat she could feel building inside of her.

"Everything I've seen so far leads me to believe I'm going to enjoy my time here very much."

"Excellent. If you need anything, please don't hesitate to contact any of our staff. We'll be more than happy to help you decide on any of the services we offer. We do have a range of treatments, especially designed for our male guests. Enjoy your stay, Mr. Whitman."

Rochelle moved away from the desk and from the man who had screwed up her equilibrium in a way she'd never experienced before.

She reached the safety of her office and closed the door. Leaning against the solid wood, she took a few deep breaths. Never before had a guest rattled her like Daniel Whitman had. She knew he was here to find out information about the resort. She would make sure she kept out of his way for the duration of his stay. If he had any questions she would refer them to her assistant, Melanie. It probably wasn't the most professional thing to do, but it was the only way she knew she could handle the situation.

For the sake of her career and to keep her focus on her lifelong goals, avoiding Daniel Whitman was a top priority now.

http://www.crimsonromance.com/upcoming-releases-romance-ebook/colleens-choice/

The Emerald Springs Legacy Series

Follow the Whitman and Sanders families in their continuing saga as they confront old rivalries and discover new love while protecting their legacy at the Emerald Tea Farm. Look for these upcoming installments in this exciting new continuity series from Crimson Romance:

Adam's Ambition by Monica Tillery
Colleen's Choice by Holley Trent
Chad's Chance by Elley Arden
Daniel's Decision by Nicole Flockton
Ashley's Allegiance by Robyn Neeley

To learn more about the Emerald Springs series, visit our website for more details, author interviews, and a special free prequel story.